A
DIFFERENT
LIE

A DIFFERENT LIE

DEREK HAAS

PEGASUS CRIME
NEW YORK LONDON

A DIFFERENT LIE

Pegasus Books LLC
80 Broad Street, 5th Floor
New York, NY 10004

Copyright © 2015 by Derek Haas

First Pegasus Books edition November 2015

Interior design by Maria Fernandez

Library of Congress Cataloging-in-Publication Data is available.

ISBN: 978-1-60598-899-3

10 9 8 7 6 5 4 3 2 1

Printed in the United States of America
Distributed by W. W. Norton & Company

For Sharon, who welcomed,

And for Ronnie, who shone.

CHAPTER

1

TRUTH DOES NOT EXIST. IT IS NOT OBJECTIVE. THERE IS
no omniscient voice that can tell you everything exactly as it happened. You are stuck with me, with my filter, seeing it unfold through
my eyes, and you will believe what I tell you to believe because it is
the only choice you have.

I'll be damned if I'm going to apologize for what's coming. You did not want the end to be the end. You asked for this. If you flinch now, well, you can rewrite it someday to better fit your sense of fairness.

Go ahead, tell my story how you want to tell it. Pass it down the way you think it should've happened. Change the ending. Save everyone. Redeem everyone. Redeem me. Make me in your image. Maybe I'd be better that way. Maybe my history will be remembered the way you write it.

But whose truth will be definitive? Yours or mine?

I've already lied to you, countless times. I will go on lying because that's what my life is, what I've practiced, what I was born into. I'm trying to change, believe me, I'm trying, but truth is the stone tied to a chain that drags a person to the bottom of the lake.

I will tell you what happened, because I need to tell someone. You can choose which parts you want to believe.

To miss another person, when it hits you, is as involuntary as blood circulating through your body. You can try to keep your mind busy, preoccupied, but the feeling, the *missing*, will seize you like an invisible fist, shaking your insides until your whole being gives in and acknowledges it. It's a powerful emotion, one I haven't understood until recently.

I am in Paris, at the Gare du Sud, waiting to meet a train. The last time I was in Paris, I botched a hit that killed two innocent people and then more who weren't so pure. I fled France in the aftermath, paying for my freedom in blood, and then escaped civilization and this life and this line of work but some dark men followed my trail and smoked me out. Dark men, government men, the kind who survive administrations by never venturing into the light. They beat me, bested me, and now count me among their number—a shooter caught in the middle, somewhere between an assassin and a spy. I'm still a contract killer, but now we use words like "sanctioned" and "high value target" and "deniability." I say "we," because Risina works alongside me.

She picks up in that last moment before I think the ringing will change to voicemail.

"Hello," she says and her voice intensifies the missing. She's Italian with just the slightest hint of an accent, but the hint is enough. It has always been enough.

"Hey, babe."

"Awww," and she calls me by my name, my real name. "I was hoping it was you."

"How is Pooley?"

"Missing his father."

"I know the feeling."

"He asked me yesterday how spiders can walk up walls."

"What'd you tell him?"

"I asked him where he saw the spider so I could squash it."

I smiled, picturing it.

"Can I talk to him?"

"He's asleep."

I looked at the big clock above the platform. "Pssh. Sorry. What time is it there?"

"5 A.M. But I don't mind, my love. I like to hear your voice."

"I miss you."

"You know what I want to hear."

"I do."

"We miss you too. How is work?"

"I'm hoping to wrap it up shortly."

"What do you need from me?"

"Your voice is what I needed."

"How is the file?"

"Impeccable."

My wife Risina is what is known in the assassination game as a fence. She stands between the shooter and the client, and she is responsible for putting together the intelligence on the target, or mark. We still use papers and maps and reports—I have no use for electronic gadgets. I'm a low-tech weapon, and I like it that way. I thought with the birth of Pooley she would fall out of this work and I'd find someone unencumbered to do the job—but Risina is a force of nature and when she insisted, I certainly wasn't going to stand in her way. Though I now work for dark men in the government, my life has not changed. They want me to kill people for money and they don't care how I do it.

My current assignment is to kill a Dutchman named Willem Kinsk. From the file Risina put together, I know the man intimately. He is forty-seven years old, grew up in Hilversum outside of Amsterdam, the son of a small-time smuggler named Anders Kinsk. He learned the business from his father, and when the old man was caught up in Interpol's net, he grabbed the reins of the family business. The father rotted away in a Belgian jail, while his son did nothing to spring him. Willem started off smuggling cigarettes, pharmaceuticals, money, and counterfeit shoes and handbags all over the continent from Holland to Serbia, England to Poland. He graduated to weapons—nothing too exotic—handguns to London, automatic rifles to Istanbul—not scary enough to merit a pixel on the CIA's radar. But the real money is in technology and when Willem facilitated a container of silicon chips from Berlin to unknown points in the Middle East, the dark men took notice. One thing I've learned in a career of killing people: if you stay inside your box, don't poke your head above the water line, you won't get your nose swatted. But the moment you expand, the moment you decide the box isn't big enough—you make yourself a target. Robert Browning once wrote "A man's reach should exceed his grasp, or what's a heaven for?" Willem should have kept his reach right where it was.

Willem's operation surpasses his old man's in both size and scope and as such, his security detail has expanded and upgraded. He employs a platoon of bodyguards from former Russian Spetznas who are properly trained and extremely professional. Files give an assassin less of a roadmap and more of an overview of how the mark lives his life—his or her strengths and weaknesses, vulnerabilities and vices, rhythms and inclinations—and from that canvas, patterns emerge. It is up to me to discover the best way to exploit those patterns.

Part of what makes me a successful killer is an ability to discover evil in my target and then feed off that evil when it comes time to finish the job. Make a connection so I can sever the connection. It's a psychological shield—an effective one—and I've built my career on its durable foundation. Kinsk is an evil man, there's little doubt. His victimless smuggling has more victims than anyone can calculate. For every drug shipment or arms shipment or silicon shipment, there are dead bodies on the other end of it, once the material makes it success-fully into the recipient's hands. I have no trouble with the evil side of Kinsk—he's a bad man and he'll meet a bad end.

Kinsk rarely steps out, preferring to stay in any of six residences around Paris—emerging from underground garages in SUVs with blacked-out windows only to stop at random restaurants or bras-series—never frequenting the same eatery twice. Then he'll head to a different apartment to spend the night, picking each residence at random. Occasionally, he'll conduct business at various warehouses near the Seine. The man is cautious in an incautious business and it has kept him alive.

I've learned—when the target is always on the move, find someone whom he meets regularly and reach that person. Discover the point where the fixed foot of the compass touches the map . . . and eventually the revolving circle will reveal that point at its center. It always does. So where is the fixed point? Risina knows there are two effective ways to locate a man who isn't looking to be found. You go through his loved ones or you find him through his vices. With some criminals, they are one and the same.

Willem Kinsk is in love . . . or at least the kind of lust that passes for love these days. The woman lives in the 3rd arrondissement in Paris in a nice three-story flat that starts at street level and goes all the way up to the roof, where she maintains a spice garden. Her name is Genevieve Forney and she is married, though not to Kinsk. She is his lover and his vice.

The key to doing my job is to always respect the details. Risina includes mention of Genevieve Forney's spice garden for a reason. She could've just called it a garden or a patio or made no mention of it whatsoever. And that's why Risina is a natural fence. The devil exploits the details.

I ring the buzzer of the unassuming flat on the rue Meslay. Like most Parisians, no one asks for the name of the visitor, there's just a mechanical "*entrer*" followed by a buzz that indicates the front door is waiting to be opened. I tug on the outer door and make my way up a short flight of stairs and knock on the address to the right. It's a building that holds just two apartments, one on each hemisphere.

A fit woman with dazzling eyes opens the door. The rest of her face might be ordinary but no one would know—it's hard to look anywhere but those eyes.

In French, she says "hello" but more as a question than a greeting. I try English. "You are Ms. Forney?"

"*Oui.*"

"We had an appointment for 11 A.M.?"

She searches her memory for some kind of recognition. "I'm sorry?"

"I am Curtis Catrell with *International Home and Garden*. Monsieur Demonte from Rivoli said he was arranging an appointment to photograph your garden. A spice garden on the roof, I understand?"

"He said nothing to me." But I already have her. Complimenting a woman's garden in Paris is akin to praising her figure. She's already swelling with pride and those eyes shine even brighter.

"I am so sorry to inconvenience you, ma'am. Demonte and I will arrange another time."

She looks at my camera bag, then back at my face. "No, no. Of course not. You want to photograph my garden? Come look. Come."

She latches on to my hand and leads me inside. The flat is more spacious than it looked from the outside, with a large open living room and a second floor that includes a master bedroom and a guest room and bath. The stairs ascend to the roof. Ms. Forney opens the door, letting in the bright light and the sweet fragrance of her garden.

"Jasmine, paprika, mint . . ."

"And rosemary, oregano . . ." I add.

"Ah, you know your gardens."

"I've shot hundreds of them. All over the world."

I move around the garden, crouching down, staring up at the sun, squatting, like I'm trying to judge the light, like I'm analyzing the photographic potential, putting on a damn good show.

"It's nice?"

"It's absolutely lovely. Is your husband home?"

She wrinkles her nose. "In Belgium."

"When will he return?"

She crosses her arms. "Why is this important?"

"Oh, we usually photograph the owners with their gardens."

I pull out the latest copy of *International Home and Garden* and flip to a spread that indeed shows a middle-aged couple in Belfast standing next to a sprout of roses. She examines it like she's afraid her answer will ruin her chances of appearing in such a prestigious periodical.

"He is out of town until next Friday."

That's good, I think. Kinsk will come some time between now and then. I just have to remain vigilant.

I smile to ease her tension. "May I come back next Saturday, then?"

She nods, relief flooding her face. Her eyes glimmer, merry. I can see why Kinsk's circle intercepts this fixed point.

I move down the street and into a chocolate shop to browse over the truffles while keeping an eye on Ms. Forney's door. This part of the job requires patience. I have the small comfort that her husband is out of town for the next six days and that the opportunity will be tempting to Kinsk, the grapes hanging low on the vine. I just have to keep Ms. Forney in sight and let her lead me to him. Kinsk might be ever-cognizant of protecting his security, but she's as guile-less and wary as a new-born fawn. She let me into her house at the cost of simple flattery. She will not be difficult to track.

I settle into a wooden chair, pull out a few pages from Risina's file, and begin to look at neighborhood maps. I'm going to have to find a way to camouflage myself on this street until she makes a move. If she leaves on foot, I'll—

I must've accidentally brushed up against a four-leaf clover in that garden, because I see a man wearing his collar up and a fedora slung low over his eyes approach Ms. Forney's door, flanked by two large foot soldiers wearing matching trench coats.

He uses a key and the trio moves inside. I have no doubt this is Kinsk, the man I'm going to kill today. I also have no doubt he's going to bolt as soon as Ms. Forney tells him the happy news that an international magazine wants to photograph her garden. His suspicion will be raised, heightened when she gives my description, and will explode off the charts when she details for him how I snooped around the apartment. She'll protest that I was a legitimate photographer and why can't he just be happy for her and why does everything always have to be so dramatic with him, and as she's talking, he'll be ordering his men to make sure their firearms are ready.

He's probably told her a lot of things but not what he really does for a living. Or at least that's what I imagine is happening in the flat right now.

Kinsk must be feeling like his lover's house is made of bricks, protecting him from the big, bad wolf, because he hasn't tried to make a break for it.

From my reconnaissance of the flat, there appears to be only one way in or out—through the front door. My gut tells me he's still inside and I trust my gut more than my eyes after a lifetime of hunting men. If he's going to try to wait me out, I will force his hand.

I pick out a piece of chocolate, pay for it, and pop it in my mouth while I cross the rue Meslay, trying to decide whether or not I should keep up the false pretense that I'm a photographer. As a general rule, I try to maintain the advantage for as long as possible; the only reason to storm the place is if I'm certain Kinsk knows a killer is coming for him. For all I know, he came home, and he and Ms. Forney climbed in the sack without bothering to talk. His bodyguards will open the door and I can smile first and quickly assess the situation or I can kick the door in and end some lives before they have a chance to mount a defense. There are benefits to both plays, but one thing I know is I can't sit around in this chocolate shop waiting to make a decision. At this moment, there are only four people in that apartment . . . if he's in there, on the phone, calling for reinforcements, that number can change quickly.

In this line of work, if you get tired or cocky, you jeopardize your assignment. You play the odds, always. You eschew risk, always. You play the cards you are dealt, always. It's one of the reasons I'm a Silver Bear. I keep my concentration high, my patience endless, and my frustration low.

I knock on the door, once, twice, in a happy cadence, my face arranged to show off my brightest smile. The sky is darkening and the moon has come out, just over the top of the adjacent building. It looks like an eye with a droopy lid, like a prizefighter in the later rounds, trying to get off the stool to answer one more bell.

I've seen this moon before.

CHAPTER

2

I'VE BEEN A HIT MAN SINCE I WAS RELEASED OUT OF juvey in Massachusetts at nineteen. A contract killer, Hap Blowenfeld, recruited me to work for an olive-skinned Italian man named Vespucci. Vespucci took my old name and cast it aside as though he were tossing out stale bread and christened me "Columbus," a new name for a new world. I grew quite adept at killing under his tutelage and have held steady employment for more than a dozen years. I met Risina a few years ago and for a short time, a very short time, I left the business and forged ahead with a new life on a beach in the Philippines. But the old ways caught up with me and I learned what so many have learned before me: once you enter the killing business, there is no exit other than death. Each contract you fulfill makes any number of fresh enemies and the pool of people who would like to see your ticket punched spreads like a flash fire.

Around the same time the government forced me into their stable, I found Risina was pregnant with our son, Pooley. My new employers, the dark men, had us over a barrel, so we decided we'd forge ahead with this arrangement: Risina as fence, me as bag man, until we could plan a proper escape. And here's a secret. We're both good at this job, we both enjoy it, and now that the threat of arrest is gone, we're comfortable with what we do. There are plenty of cops and firefighters and paramedics who leave their families at the breakfast table to perform dangerous jobs every day without a second thought.

The first job I had—sorry, *assignment* I had for the dark men involved killing a Cuban spy in New York City, a man named Yordan Abadin. Yordan's cover was as an importer, namely Cuban cigars into select clubs in the city. The Harvard Club, the DAC, the Core Club, that type of thing. Of course, a number of politicians, judges, and Wall Street millionaires were members of these fine establishments, and they all knew Yordan as a jolly and unassuming personality who slipped a Cohiba Exclusivo into the pockets of his friends. He was an effective listener and adept at getting himself invited to meetings and parties where issues were discussed. He had a way of turning the subject to his homeland without his friends realizing they'd been steered in that direction. And when a bribe or favor needed to be brokered between the Cuban government and influence peddlers, he was the one called. Analysts in the CIA, the aforementioned dark men, must've discovered his identity and decided his threat outweighed his usefulness, because he ended up landing his name at the top of one of my files.

Risina was six months pregnant at the time. I suggested a pinch hitter to serve as the fence on this one, but she refused. Said if I took this from her she would murder me in my sleep. I used to think pregnancy hormone issues were overblown until I came face to face with an Italian woman in the throes of her second trimester. Arguing with her was like staring into the jaws of a tiger.

She worked diligently and efficiently and in four weeks gave me a file with numerous ways to strike. This was a cupcake assignment, a two out of ten on the danger scale. While Yordan was an asset to his country, he had no security to speak of, no special skills, no military training in his past—he was a talker who had a good cover, who was a master of the charm offensive, and who was soft and lazy and fat. He would bleed out on his floor without putting up a fight.

After reading Risina's file, I determined the best way to dispose of Yordan would be to knock on his door—he lived alone—and when he opened it, shoot him in the forehead. And this is the part I'll emphasize: *most kills are like this.* Most aren't complex, aren't suspenseful. They're simple. The fence does all the work, and the hit man chooses the easiest path to eliminate his target and escape. Then again, sometimes the shepherd boy slays the giant with a little pebble and a slingshot.

I told Risina my plan.

"What about the back of his cigar shop?" she asked.

"What about it?"

"It's quiet. Usually empty . . ."

"Risina."

"What?"

"You're the fence. You give me the file. You make suggestions and I do the rest."

"But I spent a lot of time on it. I not only located architectural blueprints of his shop, I cased it, visited it, took pictures."

"You did, yes."

"Don't patronize me."

"What do you want me to tell you? I read your file, reviewed your choices and made the decision to strike him where he lives instead of where he works."

"Based on what?"

"I'm not going to tell you that, Risina," I said, exasperated. "We don't discuss it from here. That's the job you signed up for." She is so talented at compiling reports, I sometimes forget how new she is to this job, to this business.

"Pssssh." Her face darkened and her nostrils flared. She really is quite beautiful when she's angry, and I never mind when that anger surfaces. Maybe some small part of me pushes her buttons just to see that look on her face. "I'm not just your fence . . . I'm your wife."

"They're separate."

"They're *not!*"

The line between wife and fence in my mind is as rigid as a wall. Risina sees it more as the border on a war map, the kind that moves whenever an aggressor chooses to ignore it.

"Fine. Whatever you want," she said and then let out a stream of curses in Italian as she marched out of the room, her hands flapping wildly.

It was best to pull my troops and regroup, bring it up again when she'd blown herself out. "I'll call you when it's done," I shouted.

"Okay," she said and slammed a door somewhere down the corridor that led to our bedroom.

"Okay," I said back to an empty room.

Yordan's building was on the Upper West Side, near 65th and Broadway. It didn't have a doorman, so I wasn't going to have to worry about some elaborate ruse to remain faceless. I knew Yordan was home because I'd watched him enter the building thirty minutes before. A droopy-lidded moon had centered in the cloudless night sky, and I involuntarily shuddered looking up at it. Sometimes there are warning signs.

I knew Yordan's routine and I knew he'd answer the door when I knocked and I knew there were only three other doors in his hallway (two belonged to shut-ins and the third's owner was away on business) so I knew I could get off an anonymous shot and get the hell out of there without being discovered. I was already out the stairwell door and standing in front of Yordan's apartment, and that half-mast yellow moon was peeking through a corridor window, when I felt my phone vibrate against my thigh. Yes, I've been in this business a long time and yes, I'm a professional, at the top of the list for people who do what I do, and as a professional, I maintain complete focus when I'm on a mission. I carry a phone . . . I'd be a fool not to, but I never answer it, I never *answer*, but something about seeing that low-lidded moon had me uneasy and I made the mistake, more of a reflex actually, of slipping the phone from my pocket to check the number.

It was Risina. Risina who knew I was in the middle of an assignment. Risina who would absolutely never interrupt unless it was an emergency. I had to answer, it wasn't a choice, and as I said "hello" and she told me through ragged breaths she was going into labor, the baby was coming, it was coming right now, three months early, she told me all this in a flood of words and moans and gasps, half English and half Italian, and just as my mind processed what was happening, a premature birth, our baby rising up from her belly way too early, much too soon to be healthy and whole and safe, Yordan opened his door.

I had no idea where I was or what I was there to do. The fat Cuban started to walk out of his door with his keys in his hand, about to go get a sandwich or check his mailbox or run any of countless mundane errands, but instead he found me standing on his doorstep with a phone in my hand instead of a gun. One look at me and he knew. I don't know how he knew, but a man spying behind enemy lines as long as he had must've honed a keen danger detector, because he knew. He hopped backwards like a pheasant scampering to underbrush, and the door slammed in my face. For a man who was probably just shy of three hundred pounds, he moved very quickly, I'll give him that.

Sloppy. The one adjective I have never allowed to define my work and yet here it was. No other word seemed adequate: it was sloppy to take an assignment with my wife this far along and it was arrogant to think we were immune to pregnancy complications. My face turned red; my ears burned.

I thought for a moment about kicking his door in and completing my mission, but the dark men were going to have to deal with a snake-eyes assignment because the primal urge to care for my wife and first-born child kicked in with unyielding force. My wife was delivering a baby three months prematurely and I had to help her. I didn't know how, but I had to try. Through the hallway window, the moon's eyelid seemed to droop further, almost closed.

I turned on my heels and left Yordan's door where it was, still rattling in its hinges from the slam it received, and as I headed toward the elevator, I spoke into the phone, "Risina, listen to me. Hang up and call 911. Don't try to drive yourself to the hospital."

"Okay. Yes, yes, yes. Okay."

"I will meet you there as soon as I—"

And my voice was cut off as a bullet slammed into the elevator controls, shattering them. My phone flew and I pivoted as the impact of the bullet tossed shrapnel in my face, cutting my cheek, and I caught a glimpse of Yordan aiming a Makarov semi-automatic pistol at me, his hand shaking.

I was stunned. In all the insanity of the last thirty seconds, my mind had shut Yordan out as soon as he slammed the door in my face. I didn't think he'd find a firearm and move out of his door on the offensive. I didn't think of him at all. Yet here he was, pistol up and shaking and aimed in my direction, an elevator behind me that had no controls to summon it, a stairwell on the opposite end of the corridor, a phone gone, blood sprouting like blooming flowers from several cuts to my face, and somewhere my wife giving birth to a baby that would most likely need life support to survive.

A man doesn't need to be well trained or even semi-accurate from the short range where we stood. Surprise is always the greatest weapon in a fight, whether it's an ambush or a blindside or using a knee to the balls when your enemy thinks you will throw a hook to the face.

I'm sure Yordan thought I would fall back or hold my hands up and say "wait" or get on my knees and beg for my life. Instead, I charged. His eyes popped wide and he backpedaled and he made the rookie mistake of trying to squeeze off a round while his arms windmilled. I dodged right as the bullet sailed high into the ceiling, nowhere close to finding its target. In full stride, I leapt up, planted one foot on the wall, and then thrust forward with the hardest right cross I've ever thrown, catching Yordan flush in the ear with all of my weight behind the blow. His porcine head ricocheted off my fist and rebounded off the wall, like a one-two combination from a heavyweight. His knees gave way and his body followed them to the floor like a drunk sliding off a barstool.

I retrieved the Makarov. I couldn't remember having held one before.

If Yordan had stayed in his apartment and counted his lucky stars, I wouldn't have been holding it then. But he didn't, he came at me, and so I shot him straight through the temple, defenselessly, mercilessly, and then walked three feet and retrieved my phone off the ground. My call with Risina was disconnected and when I tried to redial, she didn't answer. I hoped she was in an ambulance, hurtling toward the hospital.

I headed for the stairwell, swiping my hand across my stinging cheek. It came back shiny and slick with blood and I realized I was breathing hard, like a sprinter after crashing through the tape. How long had it been since I entered this building? Five minutes? Ten?

I jackhammered down the stairs as sirens approached. Although I worked for the government and, if I got arrested, I was somewhat assured the dark men would find me and help me out of a jail cell, the NYPD didn't know the details of that deal and I had no patience for getting detained, not now, not today. I poked my head out of the stairwell just as two uniformed patrol officers entered, their radios squawking, and made their way toward the elevator. One of the shut-ins must've dialed emergency services when she heard the commotion in the hallway. If I kept the door cracked, I could see the cop's profiles without them returning the favor, but for how long? I couldn't kill them, or at least I didn't want to—they were innocent of this and my predator's claws were drawn in.

Miraculously, the elevator doors sprung open. I almost burst out laughing—the bullet had shattered the third-floor controls but that didn't mean the entire system was down. As soon as they stepped inside the car, the doors closed behind them and I was out of the stairwell, heading toward the door. If I flagged a taxi and the cab driver was halfway decent at his job, I could get to—

The doors popped back open just as I passed in front of the elevator. It wasn't working after all—whatever damage the bullet had done to the circuit board, it allowed the doors to open on the ground floor but wouldn't allow the car to rise. Naturally, the officers pressed the button that would re-open the doors and here we were. I kept my head down and walked toward the exit and the police seemed more annoyed with the malfunctioning elevator so they paid scant attention to me, instead shuffling toward the stairwell I'd just emerged from and I was almost out the door when I heard the bald one say "sir?"

I couldn't keep going and pretend I didn't hear. I turned to gauge the two police officers and they were in that warning stance cops all over the world adopt: shoulders slouched back, one hand on the gun strapped into the side holster, open faces that read "are we going to have a problem here?"

"Yes?"

"You live in the building?"

"No, sir. Just dropping something off . . ."

"Where?"

"Third floor. The, uh, elevator wasn't working."

They looked at each other, checking if one of them was catching a vibe. They wore matching expressions, turned-down mouths and hard eyes.

"What'd you deliver?"

"An envelope for EZ Express. You want the return label . . . I got it here . . . somewhere . . ." I started to pat my pockets.

The bald one turned, impatient. "Don't worry about it."

I nodded, itching to get the hell out of there . . . just a few more seconds and they'd be clomping upstairs and I'd be miles down the road before their thoughts turned to the man they saw leaving the—

A scream issued from somewhere up above, either ringing through the elevator shaft or down the stairwell and the three of us looked at each other as though I had suddenly sprouted horns. Someone must've entered the hallway up above and seen what was left of Yordan.

The bald cop tried to thumb his safety strap off his holster but probably hadn't drawn his weapon over the course of his career because he was slower than an earthworm. I sprang out the door, a "hey!" ringing behind me but I wasn't going to slow down or look back or break stride because I didn't want to kill these cops today. I flew past pedestrians and when I saw a break in traffic, I sliced across the grain, causing more than one taxi to squeal tires and jam brakes and lock up the road. The second "hey!" sounded farther away and the "stop!" following it even farther, and by the time I cut into an alley, I couldn't hear them at all. I blitzed out the other side onto Fifth Avenue and cut into a department store and immediately up the stairs and into the bathroom and into a stall, where I waited.

Sweat dotted my forehead and mixed with the blood on my face, the salt stinging the wounds but the pain was welcome. My wife was nearby, somewhere on this goddamn island, going through worse pain than me and it felt right, it felt honest that I should feel something too since I wasn't by her side, holding her hand, going through this with her. Our child was okay, I knew it even then, I knew it . . . because paying for the sins of the father, for my sins, was an account overdue, yes, but it wasn't going to get paid before I could hold my child in my arms. No, I knew that. I knew that if fate was going to pay me back for all I'd taken, all I'd destroyed, then it would wait until my child loved me, until I loved him, to sever that connection, to break that bond, to tear us from each other.

It was coming. Even then, I knew. But not that day.

I spooled a length of toilet paper, snapped it off, and blotted my face. Then did it again, and again, until the paper came away dry.

Once, the door opened and someone washed his hands and left. After an agonizing twenty minutes, I ventured out into the store.

An hour later, I walked into New York Hospital wearing a different shirt and pants I bought at the department store. The attendant at Registration checked my face and I'm sure thought maybe I was looking for the ER, but I gave her Risina's name and she typed it into her computer. She read something and I swear her face turned white. She quickly put up a mask she pulled out whenever she had terrible news. Maybe I had been wrong. Maybe this was the debt coming due. Maybe Risina had lost the baby.

"What is your relationship to the mother?"

"I'm the father. The boyfriend. We're not . . . we're practically married."

"She's in intensive care. I—"

But I was already sprinting up the corridor. Nurses passed as I thundered by like a deranged man. No one seemed surprised by my behavior. Maybe this was an everyday occurrence. Some loved one, panic-stricken, lurching blindly down a hallway.

I caught a glimpse of a sign that said something about Intensive Care and I pivoted that way. A surgeon was exiting an operating room, pulling his mask down and I started to ask him about Risina but then I saw past him to an open recovery room.

Risina lay inside, her wan, exhausted face turned, looking at me. What did I see in those eyes at that moment? Reproach? Anguish? Everything was mixed up in my mind . . . my nerves, which had been hopped up on worry and adrenaline since the phone buzzed in my pocket in that Upper West Side apartment were now completely shot.

I staggered toward the hospital room and when I broke the door's plane, Risina smiled. Then my eyes drifted from hers, to her chest, where she clutched something so tiny, it seemed impossible.

"Meet Pooley," she whispered. "Pooley, this is your father."

"I don't—"

"He weighs six pounds, eight ounces. Said they didn't even need to put him on a machine."

"He's a fighter," I managed.

"What'd you expect?" Risina answered wearily, but her voice was strong, happy.

I put my lips to her forehead, then did the same to my son.

"Nice to meet you, Pooley," I croaked.

Outside, a puffy cloud covered the half-lidded moon like an eye-patch, blinding it.

CHAPTER

3

I BLINK THE THOUGHTS OF THAT DAY OUT OF MY MIND, turn from the wilted moon, and concentrate on the task at hand. I'm here to kill Willem Kinsk, and the sooner I do so, the quicker I'll fly across the Atlantic again. The door opens and a strained face looks me up and down in the crack. The man barks French at me with a Russian accent, asking what I want.

What I want is for him to open the door the rest of the way, but what I say, as politely as I can muster, is that I was here earlier talking to Ms. Forney about her garden and that I have good news, but I can come back later or better yet, I'll just call her when I get back to the office.

The door closes in my face and I walk back toward the street, options scrambling in my head to plan B, plan C, plan D, when the door opens and Genevieve Forney beckons from the stoop, breathlessly. "Curtis, please, please. Come in, come in."

Maybe Kinsk's bodyguards aren't so talented after all.

I turn, feigning awkwardness. "I didn't mean to bother you again. I can—"

"Don't be silly, please, please." She gestures again that I should come inside. I shrug and trot back up the path.

As soon as I cross the threshold, the bodyguard who stuck his strained face in the doorway braces me against the wall with his forearm to my chest, his legs in a fighting stance, leaning into me with all his weight. His other hand pats me over, a casual, unprofessional sweep. The foyer is dark, poorly lit, but I can see his eyes are liquid with red veins the size of spaghetti noodles crisscrossing the whites. It all becomes clear to me—the reason Kinsk risked coming here, the reason the bodyguards aren't at their sharpest.

They're all hopping.

Kinsk is one of those bosses who has no friends outside the game and so he co-opts his employees for the task. He makes them party with him . . . a rail here, a hit there . . . and if these guards resisted at first, they have acquiesced now. I've seen it before, an employee who thinks the way to get a leg up is to ingratiate himself to his boss, that if he makes a personal connection, he will get the plum assignment, or will have his mistakes overlooked. It's dangerous, to think the man paying you is your friend.

These guys have been partying all night with the man they're supposed to protect, and now he's arrived at his mistress's house to turn the festivities from drugs to sex. I've interrupted the schedule.

The one who has me pinned to the wall is strong, and his breath comes out hot when he asks, "what's in the bag?"

"A camera," I answer.

He looks over at his partner, who is equally keyed up, and raises his eyebrows. Ms. Forney steps into the fray, her voice rising. In French, she screeches, "What're you doing? He's my guest! Imbeciles! You're embarrassing me."

The guards ignore her. They take orders from one man.

And now I see my target, as Kinsk steps into the room, summoned by the commotion.

"Who is he?" he asks.

"He's a photographer who—"

But Kinsk cuts her off with a sharp "I'm not talking to you."

She falls silent as quickly as if he'd slapped her across the face. I'm glad I see him like this, in his natural element. It's going to make what happens in the next ten minutes satisfying.

The guard holding me barks, "I can toss him, Willem." Another indication that what I concluded is true . . . he talks to Kinsk like they're buddies. "Willem" instead of "sir" or "boss."

"I don't want you to toss him. I want you to find out who he is."

I use the moment to speak, holding on to my cover with a clenched fist. "She was trying to tell you. I'm a garden photographer—"

The bodyguard slides his forearm up from my chest to my throat, so I stop talking and widen my eyes into a passable frightened expression. Through a restricted throat, I manage, "If you look in my bag—"

All of their eyes flick to the bag strapped to my shoulder, hanging loosely by my hip. It's a black nylon camera bag with a zipper top. The guard leans into my throat with more force, like the mere fact I called attention to the bag could set off an explosive inside. I start to make a gagging sound in my throat, more for the guard to remember what he's doing than from any danger of passing out, and the sound works, he knocks the bag off my shoulder and it falls to the floor.

His forearm comes off my throat as everyone looks at the bag as though it could detonate at any moment.

"He's a photographer, damn you!" Ms. Forney spits and then turns on her heels and leaves the room. No one takes his eyes off the bag.

Kinsk takes a step closer, pretending to be tough, fearless. "You are a photographer?"

"Yes. *International Home and Garden* . . . if you open the bag . . ."

"You open it."

I look at him and he glares back. He nods down at the bag. "Go ahead . . . show me."

I move slowly because this is the most important time of the confrontation. Over the course of my life, my killing life, I've discovered a truth regarding human behavior: people's actions, even your enemy's actions, mirror your own. If you act tense, the tension increases. If you behave erratically, so do the other people in the room.

If you move slowly, if you condense all your movements down to a glacier pace, then everyone's reactions do the same.

I crouch as though my knees are made of molasses, and reach for the bag. The barrel of a gun nudges the base of my head, where my neck meets my skull. Through my peripheral vision I see that Kinsk holds the pistol.

"Do it," he commands.

Slowly, slowly, I unzip the top. I reach into the bag and withdraw, gingerly, a Leica V-Lux point-and-shoot camera with a 50-millimeter lens and a CF-22 compact attachable flash. Everyone breathes out at once.

And here's why I slowed it all down: with everything creeping along at a snail's pace, a sudden outburst of sound or light or movement will have that much more impact when it begins.

I turn the camera up and pop the flash right into Willem Kinsk's eyes. He blinks, which is enough. A good assassin doesn't have to bring a weapon to the kill; he gets the target to brandish his weapon so he can get past the friskers and take the weapon *from* him.

I have his pistol out of his hand and into mine before anyone's speed can ramp back up. The first shot is delivered to the bodyguard who braced me. From my angle on the ground shooting up, I catch him through the fleshy part of his throat and send a chunk of his head into the crown molding that lines the entryway. The flash of the gun achieves the same effect as the flash of the camera bulb, and the second guard raises his hand to shield his eyes. The second bullet tears through his palm and into his eye socket, lifting him off his feet and dropping him to the floor next to me.

Kinsk, whose drug-enhanced mind finally processes what is happening, turns and flees for the living room like a mouse scampering for his hole when he hears the cat's purr. I don't mind shooting marks in the back; truth be told, I prefer it. It means they're not firing back at me. There is no heroism in what I do, no code, just pure calculation.

I hit Kinsk with two shots, one in the middle of his back, severing his spine, the second, a slight bit off from where I aimed, but just as effective, in the shoulder, near the heart. He drops to the floor, still breathing. I rise and step into the living room. He won't live more than a few minutes now, but I can't leave until he's dead, so I have one more shot to make to end this.

When I cross into the room, movement near the kitchen catches my eye. It's the mistress, Genevieve Forney, and I can only imagine what I look like. I've got a mask of blood peppered to the side of my face and I'm standing over the man she planned to sleep with this afternoon, his gun in my hand.

Our eyes lock and she freezes, her body stiffening like she's paralyzed. Only her mouth opens.

"You're not a photographer," she says, disappointed.

<hr />

Names bubble up from the depths of this business, rise to the surface, and pop. *Castillo, Castillo*. Pop, pop.

I've heard this name a few times over the last eighteen months. The death of a federally protected witness in Phoenix. The murder of a state senator in Biloxi. An ambassador in Chile. A businessman in Florence.

I hear he's young, barely an adult, eighteen? Nineteen? I hear he has boyish features and an everyman build. That he can slip in and out of any location: a courthouse, an office building, a fishing village, a nightclub, and no one will remember him or know he was there. I hear he can speak all the Latin-based languages, fluently.

Castillo.

They're attributing the Guantanamo tragedy to him. A marine private walked into a room of officers at the Guantanamo Bay Detention Camp, pulled the pin on a grenade, and blew himself and six fellow jarheads to kingdom come. One of the marines who died that day was Corporal Blake Hanover, son of Kurt Hanover, CFO of Boeing Corporation. It was deemed a tragedy, and the story ran for several weeks on all the news channels until the oxygen gave out and the commentators found juicier flesh to sink their teeth into. The private's name, Dennis Owen Rafferty, was plastered everywhere, and military psych records were produced, showing he was suffering from a cocktail of neuroses and diagnoses.

A lone psychopath already on the inside is easy to understand. An unstable soldier who had access to the armory, weapons provided by his country, and clearance to walk inside makes for a tidy tale. How can you protect against that?

More difficult to explain would be a hired contract killer infiltrating one of the most secure facilities in the world, hitting six active-duty servicemen while they played a card game on their cots, and then escaping in the dead of night.

Castillo.

Pop, pop.

I hear he's a lot like me.

The dark men, somewhat ironically, like to meet in well-lit, populated, noisy establishments. I'm sure the choice arises from the popularly held notion that bad things won't happen in public places. Not true. Some of the worst atrocities of our day are committed in open markets, malls, shopping centers, schools . . . with the sun shining. Still, whatever gives these men the illusion of security is fine with me.

I enter Michael's on 55th Street, a spacious white-tablecloth restaurant with a wide range of patrons, from tourists to music executives to businessmen to old-school Manhattanites in for an omelette and a bagel.

Two men wait for me in the corner, their backs to the wall, looking out at the restaurant, forcing me into the third chair, the one facing the wall. I don't like it, but I'm not going to let them know that. I sit down as if it is the exact chair that I want to sit in, and make a mental note not to check over my shoulder.

The rounder of the two men is named Cargill. I've met him before. Everything about him is round: his eyes, his head, his mouth, as if he had been composed by an artist using only a compass. He pronounces his words carefully, precision important to him.

His partner is new, though I met him the last time. His name is Lavender. If he says more than one word this time, it'll be a record.

I ask a waiter for coffee and scrambled eggs before turning my eyes to the government men.

"Nice work in Paris," Cargill offers and Lavender grunts his agreement. They have half-eaten pancakes and French toast in front of them and Lavender does that thing where he's trying to clear some food stuck in his teeth by swishing water in and out of the gaps, all while looking straight-forward, as though he's not concentrating on his dental work but giving me his full attention.

I say "It could have been more efficient," and the truth is, I'm right. It could have been. I killed four people when it should have only been one. Opportunity knocked and I struck before it slipped away. I didn't mind the bodyguards—they knew the dangers when they signed up for the work, but Genevieve Forney's murder bothered me more than it should. She was cheating on her husband, sure, but the French have always had a blasé attitude toward infidelity. Did she think it would cost her her life? I doubt it ever crossed her mind.

Cargill and Lavender let the comment drop without poking at it. Cargill checks over my shoulder and gestures at his partner with a round hand, like "get on with it" and Lavender coughs and reaches into his briefcase and hands me a file.

It's funny, in this day and age of electronic correspondence, I've found the government has gone back to its roots for its dirty laundry: hand-typed, single-copy memos created on a manual typewriter. No electronic footprint, nothing to be paraded in front of congressional committees when computers are snatched up and ripped apart to give up their secrets. Typed pages, no fingerprints.

Lavender hands me the manila folder and after the waiter breezes by with my coffee and eggs, barely looking down as he flits to the next table with an armful of breakfast plates, I open it and read the page inside. It still gets me excited, this moment when I get to first lay eyes on the name of my next mark.

Castillo.

The shortest page I've ever received from the dark men. Just a single name, a single word, actually, typed on an old Smith-Corona.

"Any confusion?" Cargill asks.

I close the file, sit back, and shake my head.

There are probably a million people in the world who share the surname Castillo, maybe more, but there is only one whose name keeps rising to the surface.

Pop, pop.

Cargill and Lavender leave a hundred-dollar bill on the table, wipe their hands on black napkins, and leave, business concluded.

I get up, move over to the seat facing the restaurant, slide my eggs over, and dig in.

Pooley's in the bathtub when I get home and he breaks into a smile and beats the water with his palms, splashing drops all over Risina and then we're laughing and I'm down on the floor, holding Risina tight while Pooley makes it rain and I can't think of any place I'd rather be than right here, right now.

"Okay, okay, hey, hey!" Risina chuckles, "that's enough. Yeah, your daddy likes to stir you up, doesn't he?"

"I live to stir you both up."

She helps Pooley climb out of the tub and towels him off. "And now your father's going to clean up this floor, isn't he? Isn't he? Uh-huh. He sure is."

"Uh-huh!" the boy crows. Risina drops the towel on me and heads toward Pooley's bedroom to help with his PJs. I watch them walk off and try to take the picture in my head and store it away for a time when I'm not this happy.

Are you judging me yet? Are you asking yourself how a man who has blood on his hands can try to be a loving father to a three-year-old? You won't get an easy answer. There isn't one. I know because I've asked myself the same question every day since Risina said "I'm pregnant."

After Pooley is fed and in bed, Risina and I sit up at the kitchen table, drinking beer, the file in front of us. Or, more accurately, the name.

"Castillo. What do you know about him?" she asks.

"Hearsay. Stories. Rumors."

"Such as . . ."

"Do you know a Spanish fence named Ramon Aiza?"

Risina shrugs. This is a common trait of Risina's . . . rather than admit *I don't know him*, she shrugs, meaning *maybe I do, maybe I don't*. Risina likes to know it all. Another reason she's a great fence and why I won't play card games with her. She admits to nothing.

"Well, Aiza is a heavy hitter in Europe, very careful, very stealthy, the perfect fence."

Risina's mouth turns down. I press on. "He has a stable of maybe a half-dozen bag men, and the youngest is this kid, Castillo. Supposedly, he's under twenty. Guantanamo was him. Supposedly. AMSCAP was him. Supposedly."

"This is a lot of *supposedly*."

"Which is why I'm prone to believe it. *Supposedly* is an assassin's bread and butter. If it can be verified, then the killer can be caught. And no one else is stepping forward to take credit."

"Hmmm."

"I'll give you one I heard directly from Aiza."

"When were you with Ramon Aiza?"

"Recently. Don't worry about it."

Risina folds her arms across her chest and her lower lip protrudes. I touch her arm. "I only have eyes for you, baby."

"You better."

I actually think she'd be more upset if I cheated on her with another fence than with another woman.

"Do you want to hear this or not?"

She shrugs. She knows I love to tell stories and she knows she loves to hear them, but she's not going to give an inch right now.

"So Ramon Aiza has a job to take out a special detective in Dublin, a guy named Braden or Brody or Brogen . . . something bruh and Irish."

Risina nods at me to get on with it.

"As luck would have it, when Aiza is out gathering information for a file on this guy, the mark chokes on a boiled chicken in the middle of dinner at a place called The Winding Stair just off the Liffey. Aiza watches it happen. He's shadowing this poor fat Irish cop and the guy is stuffing his face, and the next thing he knows, O'Braden turns beet-red and his hands go to his throat and he keels over backwards, and everyone, including Aiza, just stands around gaping, and finally the cook comes racing out of the kitchen, but O'Bannon is, as I've said, quite chubby and his back is on the ground and the cook couldn't get him into position for the Heimlich. So he turns purple and by the time the ambulance rumbles up the street, he's dead."

Risina nods. I've got her now.

"Aiza sticks around long enough to watch the paramedics struggle to get the mark's corpse into the rig and whisk him away, then he books the next flight back to Madrid because this job went sour. And this is a setback for any fence with a big job on the books because whatever fees you were gonna get just went bye-bye. The mark died of natural causes before the contract went into effect . . . good luck for the client, bad luck for the fence.

"So Aiza returns and arranges to meet Castillo or maybe they don't meet but just get in contact with each other, I can't remember, but anyway, Aiza tells him the job has evaporated and he'll need to wait for the next gig. Castillo asks Aiza for the file on Brannon. That was it, Brannon. Fat Irish cop named Brannon who dodged execution only by snuffing himself out on a chicken bone. And Aiza says you don't need to see the file, there is no file, because there is no job, because the target is dead. I watched it with my own eyes. I saw him keel over and turn purple and die. Unless he can hold his breath for eleven minutes, the target is dead. And Castillo just nods and says 'uh-huh, uh-huh, uh-huh, let me see the file.'"

I lean back in my chair.

"So Aiza is lighting up when he tells me this, like even though you know where this is going, you don't know where this is going. The telltale heart of a great story.

"Aiza forks over the file and Castillo walks off with it . . . the fence telling him he'll contact him soon for the next gig and Castillo, this brash young Spanish assassin just waves at him like 'yeah, yeah' and heads off into the night.

"Three weeks later, he comes back to Aiza and asks for a green light to collect his fee. Aiza tells him there is no fee. There is no client. The target died. Castillo just hands him a digital camera. Aiza looks at him like *what d'ya want me to do with this*, but Castillo just waits, staring at him. Aiza turns the camera over and begins to flip through the pictures on the digital screen. The first shows a very-much-alive Brannon, now with a beard and mustache, walking down a sidewalk. The second shows him in front of a boat. The third one at a bar . . . you get the idea.

"Aiza looks up, says he feels like he's got about a dozen eggs all over his face, and Castillo just stares at him with sniper eyes. 'Do I have the green light?' Aiza says he's nodding before he even knows what he's doing. He calls the client to cover his ass, you know, and the client says something about thinking the target was already dead and Aiza has to explain that it was one of those witness protection, eraser type things where the target faked his own death. And the funny thing is Aiza has no idea how this guy did it. He watched him choke. He watched the fat body go limp and stay limp for fifteen minutes. He was in the same room. Nothing in this guy's file indicated he was David Copperfield—"

"Who?"

"A magician, it doesn't matter. Houdini, then. But Aiza does the tap dance with the client and they confirm they still want this detective dead for whatever reason.

"A couple of days later, Castillo comes back and tells Aiza it's done. Aiza asks for confirmation and Castillo just stares at him, pissed. Aiza shrugs and says the client is going to need verification . . . *whapppp*, Castillo slaps him flat across the face."

I slap my hand on the table as I say it, making Risina jump. But she smiles at me.

"Aiza isn't used to getting slapped, and he isn't used to feeling scared: in fact, he can't remember the last time he actually worried if he was going to make it out of a room alive. But here he is, his cheek raw and pink and his neck hairs standing straight up, eyes locked with this young assassin. And Castillo just points to him and says, 'Pay me. Now.'"

"Aiza walks over to a safe and thinks for half a second about making a play for the pistol he tucks away in there, but instead he withdraws whatever the fee is and hands over the cash to Castillo and the young man counts it, turns, and heads out without another word. Aiza tells me he breathes out a sigh of relief and then starts thinking about ways he can get out of being Castillo's fence. I mean, it's a delicate situation here . . . the assassin is obviously very good, there is mileage to be gained from this story, whatever it says about Aiza's fencing skills is irrelevant . . . this is a good kill. An A-list kill. If you hire Castillo, the target is assured to be dead, you know?"

Risina nods . . . she does know. A kill like this would make a Silver Bear out of anyone.

"The only problem is Aiza doesn't have a body, he's never had a body other than the one he watched go into the back of an ambulance. And that one was fake. Now he has to call and tell the client that the deal is done, the target has been killed, again, there is no proof but to take his word for it. The client has to think this is some kind of scam going on by now, right?

"So Aiza thinks about eating the fee, about wiping his hands of the whole mess, maybe he's getting too old or careless for this job anyway. So he turns out the light, shuts the door, and walks down to his car, thinking all sorts of morose thoughts . . . he pops his trunk to put his briefcase in back and the smell hits him and he reels back and lying there in his trunk is the bloated, dead body of one Irish police special detective Brannon staring back at him."

Risina looks at me for a long time, inscrutable, then shakes her head. "Damn."

"I know," I say.

She leaves for Spain the next day. She has two to three weeks to put together a file on the best way to kill Castillo and then I have five to six weeks to complete the assignment. We aren't much on good-byes. Saying the word is unlucky.

I take Pooley to the High Line park in the West Village, an old railroad spur blight transformed over one and a half miles into a peaceful, gorgeous garden complete with plants, art, benches, and views, a modern triumph of human imagination.

I sit in a patch of grass and let Pooley sprawl in the sunshine and on the street below I hear two cars screech their brakes, blast their horns, and one of the drivers yells "go fuck yourself."

CHAPTER

4

I STAND IN FRONT OF *GUERNICA*, PICASSO'S HAUNTING canvas, perhaps the greatest artistic indictment of modern warfare ever created, and think of how I'm going to kill Castillo. Risina's file is as baffling as it is thorough. She certainly has uncorked several avenues to reach him, but as far as finding him herself, giving me any information regarding his personal life, his routines, his relatives, his whereabouts? These are absent.

This is a first. She usually hands me a file and after I have a chance to absorb it, we talk for a day or two about things on which I might need further clarification. Or I might home in on a line of attack and ask her opinion regarding intricate details.

When she handed me this file, she didn't look me in the eye. She passed it off with a wrinkled nose as if the paper itself were contaminated. As if she were ashamed.

I didn't press her. Time is always a factor, so from the moment she returns to the moment I leave, we rarely overlap for more than a day or two. As I dug into the documents, usually my second favorite part of any assignment, I began to understand Risina's failure. She volunteered no excuses for why she had come up empty, and I knew complaining to her about it would be akin to rabbit-punching ribs that were already broken.

So instead I focused on what *was* in the file, thirty pages on Castillo's fence, Ramon Seguin Aiza. I thought about asking Risina why she led with this information, why she clearly thought the best way to get to Castillo was through his middleman, but I'm not sure I want to pull back that particular curtain. If Risina has a flaw, it's her competitive nature. Would she expose the weaknesses in someone else's fence just because it's too good an opportunity to pass up? Would she do it all the more because she was unable to put eyes on the target himself? Or was she able to check her emotions and concentrate on the single best avenue to eliminate Castillo?

Museum-goers enter and exit the *Guernica* room in waves, a tour group here, a couple of seniors there, a cluster of school kids holding on to a long piece of yarn like dogs tied to a sled. One boy stops and stares at the bottom of the canvas, where Picasso painted a corpse lying on the ground, a broken knife in his hand, his arms sprawled. Another figure in the painting extends a candle from a window above, but the light does not make it to the man.

The boy's mother grabs him under the elbow and leads him away. He throws another glance over his shoulder at the canvas, eyes wide, mouth frowning, and then he's gone. Maybe they'll stop longer in front of Velasco's *Adam and Eve.* I've often wondered why parents bring kids to art museums. Even the religious paintings are filled with bloody thorns and spear gashes and nailed hands on crosses. There's more murder than water lilies, that's for sure.

Aiza lives in Cortez, just off the Huertas, walking distance from here. He once had an office in nearby Letras, but has winnowed his client list down to a half-dozen killers and subsequently gave up his office and whatever protection it afforded. He now meets his clients in tapas bars around the city. He is sure no one knows where he rests his head, in a second-floor flat on the Calle Cadiz, above a toy store. I wonder how Risina acquired the address. I'll have to ask her when this is done.

I think about setting up a meeting as I've done before, pretend interest in taking an assignment from him, let him pick the meeting place. While I think I could surprise him with my true purpose, I don't want to be on his mind. I have his home address, and ambushing a man in the place he feels safest remains one of the most effective ways to reach a target.

His apartment is indeed above a store that sells handcrafted wooden toys: cars, planes, trains, robots, dolls. The street smells like sawdust and I imagine an old gray-haired woodcutter making the toys on the premises. I can't help but smile. I saw Pooley playing with a wooden biplane before I left. Now I know where he got it.

On the second floor, Aiza's light goes out and a few moments later he emerges from a door next to the shop, looking like a squat beaver heading out from the dam to find some fresh tree branches.

He doesn't have the darting eyes, the paranoid sweeping gaze of most of the fences I know. Maybe he never had it.

I have a decision to make. I can break into his apartment and wait for him to return, or I can follow him and see where he's going. The first plan is sound, because he didn't leave with a suitcase or so much as a backpack, so he'll be returning soon. Risina's file indicates he likes to conduct business in the morning, then eat a midday meal in his apartment, after which he takes a short nap. The sound, sensible plan is to wait for him in his closet, and emerge right when he takes off his pants, folds his shirt neatly and hangs it from the bedpost. Catch him completely off-guard, when he's at his most vulnerable. That's definitely what I should do.

The other choice is to follow him and see what business he has to conduct.

I'm curious. I've met with many fences over the years, from the most secretive and cautious to men so lazy and careless they were an embarrassment to the profession. I never got that vibe off of Aiza. He seems to me somewhere between the extremes. He takes his profession seriously but doesn't let it make him paranoid. Maybe Risina saw this in him and envied it. Or resented it.

I follow him down the street and he gives no indication he knows I'm there. I've always been strong at this part of the game, keeping a mark in my sightline without showing my face. There is something innate in humans, when you feel a man's face pointed your way, your awareness heightens. You know he's there. You are drawn to turn your head and confirm it. Carl Sagan called it the shadow of forgotten ancestors, evolutionary survival-of-the-fittest imprints passed down in our genes from the time we were cavemen protecting our clan. A killer can counteract this survival instinct, this power of fear, by never pointing his face directly at his mark. Stay in the shadows, keep your head pointed up, down, off-line, whatever direction the mark is and keep him in your sightline through window reflections or by training your eyes to capture a wider field of vision. With a little practice, you can take in specific details located only in your periphery.

So I shadow Aiza and he strolls along the Huertas, not a care in the world. He stops, checks an address on his phone, then heads up and disappears inside an apartment building. I google the address but nothing jumps and I'm certain Risina did not mention it in her notes. Whom he's meeting and for what purpose are unknown.

Again, I have a choice. I can follow or retreat, and this time, the smart play wins out. I have no business going into that building. I'm not sure why I even went this route to begin with . . . I've gotten as far as I've gotten by making the reasoned choices.

It takes me less than ten minutes to pick my way back to Aiza's apartment. I find myself chewing on the inside of my lower lip to the point where I feel pain. Why did I just waste the last half hour following my target? Why didn't I do the smart thing right from the get-go? If I had to guess, I'd say my concentration flagged. I'm not even halfway to killing my target . . . this is the man who will lead me to the man, after all . . . and yet the ease with which I got to him dipped my focus. No more. I'm going to break into his loft and sit in a chair and wait for him to return. When he does, I'm going to persuade him to help me contact Castillo.

I cross the street and am thinking about whether I'm going to pick the lock to his building entrance or trick someone into buzzing me in, when I'm knocked off my stride by two thick men, shoved through a door, and knocked into a stand of wooden puppets, shelves crashing down on top of me. My brain works just fast enough to realize two things: namely, Aiza isn't as carefree and foolish as I imagined, and his bodyguards are professionals.

Before I can untangle myself, the stouter of the two men kicks me hard under the elbow, toe to ribs, and my hope is he didn't crack any bones, though I can't be sure. I feel myself fighting for air and a second blow comes as soon as I lower my arm, this time toe to shoulder, which sends my whole body into a second set of shelves.

Usually, when I fight, I'm able to overpower my assailant because I'm willing to do things undignified. Scratch the eyes, kick the balls, bite the neck, punch the kidneys again and again because the fights I find myself in mean the victor walks away and the loser dies. These guys are cut from the same cloth. As soon as I dip my shoulder to protect my ribs, the larger one goes down on one knee and starts driving his fist into the side of my unprotected head. I snarl at him, try to get my teeth into his flesh, his knuckles, anywhere, but he doesn't stop.

I feel an eruption of pain in my groin, and the world goes bright white, and then, mercifully, dark.

The pain is everywhere. It rolls in waves, synced with my heartbeat, so every two seconds, a fresh blanket of barbs wraps around me. My chest, my arms, my legs. Kick, kick, kick. Beat, beat, beat. Barb, barb, barb.

Then in the darkness, a hard slap across my face that rattles my teeth. Someone knows I am conscious and wants me to open my eyes. I check my wrists first and yes, they're bound by rope, same with my ankles, though I have about an inch of wiggle room there. Before I get cracked again, I open my lids and take in the room.

I'm in what must be the back room of the toyshop, a large space with no windows, a workbench running the length of one wall and a pegboard filled with every woodworking tool hung from hooks: planes and levels and sanders and drills and bits and hammers and saws.

Aiza sits across from me, in a metal folding chair, the twin of the one I'm in. One of his heavies is behind him, at the end of the workbench, his eyes on me. The other is behind me somewhere, in the shadows. I can hear him breathing.

Aiza folds his hands over his belly and eyes me with a frown, his head back, his chin disappearing into his neck. He makes a *tsk, tsk* sound, clucking his tongue like a disappointed parent. "You think I didn't know you were coming, Columbus?"

I've learned when someone wants to talk, let him.

"Such arrogance. I know all. I know everything." He pauses, waiting to see if I'll fill in the gap. When I don't, he adds, "So someone wants me dead. Before you leave here today, or, better to say, before your *body* leaves here today, I will find the answer to that question. So, so, so. Okay."

He cranes his neck to look back at the stout one. I can't see it, but he must signal him with his eyes, because the bodyguard moves to the pegboard, selects a wood planer, and takes it off its hook. He hands it to Aiza and the fence sets it on his knee, his head still back so he's looking at me over the arch of his nose. He looks like an otter on his back, picking at an oyster.

"Okay, okay. So you should know, Columbus, my father owned this toy store, God rest his soul. I grew up using these tools. The sawdust would get in my eyes, my ears, my hair. But I loved it. I loved my father and I loved this shop and I loved the sawdust. I probably used this wood plane a thousand times. You want to see how it works?"

He hoists himself out of the folding chair with a youthful spring, more energy than I thought he had, and shuffles over to the workbench. He finds an uncut block of wood, a 2 X 4, and holds it up in the light for me as though to say, *you see?* Next, he sets it on top of the workbench and, with the sure hands of experience, rolls the tool over the length of the block. A curlicue of shaving rolls out of the top of the wood block like an apple peel.

"Now imagine this wood is the flesh of your arm, okay? Your stomach, yes?" He waddles back to me and sits again in the same position, the plane bouncing on his knee like a newborn. He eyes me for a moment, his breath coming in and out of his nose in a rough wheeze, and though some small part of me wants to see how far he'll take this, the larger part screams not to test him. He's a fence who made it a long time in the killing world, long enough to acquire the silver hairs on top of his head, so no, best not to test him.

"I'm not here to kill you," I say.

Aiza chuckles. "Oh, I see, I see. You have your fence stalk me for eight weeks? What? You think I would not spot her? Arrogance. So much arrogance. I've been doing this a long time, Columbus. I've seen everything. You then show up yourself to finish the job, okay? Follow me all the way down the Huertas, then backtrack to my house to what? Offer me a nice bottle of wine? No, you aren't here to kill me. You just want to talk, is that it? You want to write my life story? Okay. Well, here you go. Chapter one. The man I'm writing about is smarter than me. Chapter two. He killed me when—"

"Are you going to shut up so I can finish?"

He stops, and now a little fire lights up his eyes. I don't let him respond, just continue with, "I'm tired, I'm sore, I'm a little thirsty if I'm being honest, so I'd like to get to my purpose so we can put this stupid torture business aside and get to the nitty-gritty."

He tips his chair back now so he can look even further down the length of his nose at me. Then he spreads his hands as though to say *continue, continue.* The wood plane bobs on his knee like a fussy toddler.

"I'm here to kill Castillo. I don't know how to get to him. My fence couldn't get to him. I was coming to you to see if you wanted to deal. If that's the case, then let's deal. If not, let's get on with it."

He looks over my shoulder at the bodyguard behind me, but I can't see what unspoken communication passes between them. The plane stills. Aiza scratches his beard with chubby sausage fingers and clears his throat. "A fence gives up his stable, he gets a bad reputation."

"Even so, there it is. I'm going to kill Castillo. You want to help me, help me."

He sets his chair down on all four legs, gets up, and waddles over to the pegboard. He hangs the plane in its spot and this time selects an old manual sander. Aiza runs it over the 2 X 4, smoothing down the place he just planed. If he wants to think it over, I'll let him. Aiza bends over as much as his waist will allow and blows off the sawdust.

"You know what I like most about this old store? Each block of wood could become anything you wanted it to be. It starts with just this uninteresting rectangle, a plain old brick, but in my father's hands? In my father's hands it became a clown or a truck or a gun or a space ship. Anything."

I can't help myself. I really am thirsty. So I interrupt with, "Actually, it started as a tree if we're gonna get technical."

The fire leaps up in his eyes again. It's kind of fun to watch. I've interrupted his stupid philosophizing, and he doesn't like it. He wags his finger at me. "You're not good enough."

He starts back toward me. "I spotted your fence a mile away. I planned for you, prepared for you, and now here you are, incapacitated in my father's toyshop, trying to make a deal with your mouth. But you're not good enough. Castillo will eat you alive. And then he would come for me."

"You're afraid of him."

"I'm not a gambler, Columbus. I never have been. I'm a planner. I see a block of wood and I turn it into a toy. I turn that toy into money. It's simple. You can't kill Castillo, even if I pointed you to his doorstep. Okay? So . . . so, so, so."

"But you can't control him. And that's more dangerous to a planner than anything else. An uncontrollable variable. I'll take care of him for you."

"You're not listening, Columbus. You may have been up for it once, but you're not that man anymore. I knew it the last time we sat down. I thought when we ordered the first course I would make a play for you, but by the time dessert came, I thought, why bother? There's a shelf life to your side of things, friend. It's like a football player. He can't run the pitch in his thirties the way he could in his twenties. Younger players replace the older ones. I'm sorry. It's the way it is."

He nods at the guy over my shoulder, which is what I've been waiting for. These guys have seen too many movies where the guy chained to the chair is surprised by the man standing behind him who slices his throat with a razor. I thought it would come sooner, actually.

I feel fingers reach into my hair at the top of my head in order to pull my chin back, to expose my neck.

The problem with chaining someone's ankles to a chair, particularly with rope instead of proper leg irons, is the victim can push his weight forward and stand. As soon as the fingers touch my hair, I wrench forward with all my strength and get my feet flat on the floor, the chair tied to me so I'm in a kind-of quasi-crouched position. Surprise is on my side.

I plow backwards into the man who was about to slit my throat, driving him into the wall using the chair's legs like a battering ram, and the brace of the chair catches him in the gut and he doubles over so his head comes down even with mine and I rear back and smash my temple into his. He drops, writhing, and I take a quick glance across the room.

Aiza is so astounded by this turn of events that all he can do is gape, but the bodyguard behind him pulls his firearm as he is trained to do. I have about five seconds and if physics don't work in my favor, then this was all for naught and I might as well have given up my neck. My thoughts should remain clear but they drift to Pooley in that bathtub, that laughter, the water splashing on the floor and even with my ankles roped to the chair, I hop into the air, no more than a few inches but enough to shift my weight and crash backward and down, like a man doing a cannonball from the side of a swimming pool. I drop hard on to the stone floor with the entire weight of my body on the seat of the chair.

Water splashing on the floor. Bubbles drifting up, popping at the surface. Laughter. Pop, pop.

And then the sound in the room kicks back in and I hear the guard I headbutted moaning. I try an arm and sure enough, the metal folding chair has split and my left hand and both feet are free. I hear a gunshot and a bullet careening off the cement, low and skipping over my head. Before he can fire again, I lurch to the writhing guard's body and scramble behind it, ignoring the sharp pain from whatever the metal chair did to the small of my back. The next shot is low again, and it plugs into the writhing guard's rib cage. This happens quite a bit . . . gunmen practice shooting at ranges with targets positioned straight across from them. They rarely practice shooting at objects rolling on the ground.

The writher's body reacts like a worm poked with a knife; he flops up on his elbows and knees, then flat again, then up again in quick succession. In doing so, he exposes his holster.

My right hand is still attached to the remains of the folding chair, but with my left I flick open the button on the safety strap and pull the guard's pistol. No, not his pistol. A Glock 17. *My* Glock 17 this asshole took and tucked away like it was a spoil of war. He's still flopping and bending like that stuck worm, and I can hear his breath wheezing on every inhale so I shoot him at close range through the heart and his movement stops. Better. He was about to expose me with all that movement but now he's like the sandbags at the top of a World War I trench, and I lie flat behind him, using his back as a prop for my left hand so I can aim.

Some people live their lives like it's made of minutes. A few of us know it's the split seconds that count.

The other bodyguard has come alongside Aiza, who sits as before, gaping. The bodyguard's confidence is shot, that's as easy to read as a Hardy Boys mystery. He has his gun pointed at me, but he's unsure about pulling the trigger again.

"So," I say.

Aiza finds his voice. "Okay, okay, okay. I was wrong. Hold it. *Para ya!* Hold it." He has his hands out in front of him, palms up, as if he can push the last forty-five seconds back into a bottle. "Let's talk, Columbus. You came here to talk."

"I thought we *were* talking."

The bodyguard with the gun pointed at me throws a glance at Aiza, incredulous. Incredulous that he could resume negotiations after the explosion of violence he just witnessed. His eyes quickly jump back to mine.

"Okay, okay." Aiza seems to rely on that word like a tic. "Okay, Columbus, I see now why you have the reputation you have. I heard, but now I see. Okay. Seeing is a different thing. You say you can take care of Castillo, I see that you can. Okay."

The bodyguard's face is now screwed into an expression of open disgust. *How can he be capitulating to this bastard who killed my partner,* it asks. Aiza doesn't seem to notice.

"You give me everything you have on him," I say, "and we both walk out of here."

"Yes, okay. Deal. We have a deal."

"I'm going to stand up now, then we're going to put away our guns and get down to business. But I tell you right now, Aiza, if your man there gets jumpy, I'm going to plug both of you and find another way."

"No, no. Okay. No." Aiza seems to notice his armed bodyguard for the first time. He raises his hand to him as if to tell him to calm down. "Miguel. Lower your arm, you stupid pig."

Miguel's eyes flash and I keep my gun trained on him but I work myself up to my feet. He still hasn't lowered his weapon.

"Miguel!" Aiza beseeches. "It's okay, you whore dog."

Miguel's voice is thin. "He killed Philippe."

"Well, to be accurate, you shot him first," I offer, which is probably not helpful to this situation, but I'm starting to come down from the adrenaline and every part of my body aches. Equally, I'm growing weary of this asshole's gun pointed in my direction.

Finally, Miguel lowers it. Aiza shakes his head like he still can't figure out how this situation went sideways, but here we are, that hand's been played, and it's time to reshuffle the deck.

Except Miguel slides behind Aiza and puts his gun to his boss's temple.

"What are you doing?" Aiza stammers but Miguel cuts him off with a brusque "Shut up! *Cayate!*" Then, to me, "I'll kill him."

I don't say anything. I haven't lowered my gun, even when he did his.

Aiza tries again. "Miguel, quit being a pathetic cow. He's—"

"I said shut up!" Miguel spits. "He killed Philippe! He'll kill us too!"

Again, he turns to me, as though the two conversations are taking place in different rooms. "We're backing out of here. This fat fuck has information you need, yes? Well, you can get it when I'm safely away."

Miguel keeps most of his body hidden behind Aiza, with just one eye peeking out of the side of his boss's neck. "Now, *jefe*, here we go.

Slowly. And if you make a move I swear to Mary, Joseph, and all the saints, I will kill this man."

Aiza reluctantly backs toward the door, a human shield for the man who was hired to protect him, and they backpedal in a clumsy choreographed dance. A gunshot from a 9mm handgun, like the one I hold in my hand, puts out about 160 decibels when fired. To put that in perspective, a chainsaw runs about 100 decibels. A police siren is about 120. Combine that with a room with a concrete floor, no windows, low ceilings, and not a lot of furniture to dampen the sound, and I have enough shock and awe in my hand to make a deaf man flinch. I have to hope that flinch won't manifest in Miguel's trigger finger blowing Aiza's head off his shoulders, but if it happens, so be it.

I aim a foot over Aiza's head and pull the trigger. The shot reverberates in the room as if lightning struck the back wall and Aiza jerks like someone poked him with a cattle prod, exposing Miguel. My second shot isn't as loud as the first, or maybe it's just because my ears are ringing, but the bullet finds its target, and the back of Miguel's head splashes against the wall.

I didn't aim low.

Aiza and I sit in a bay window of the Casa Gonzalez, a plate of charcuterie, Iberian ham, and manchego cheese in front of us. The dead bodies of his two protectors lying in the sawdust of the wood shop will be taken care of, he assures me, right before he says "let's eat." It turns out nothing, not even sudden twists of fate, come between Aiza and his midday meal.

"Now to Castillo," Aiza says between bites. "Who wants him clipped?"

I shrug.

Aiza clucks his *tsk, tsk* again and wags his finger. "I disrespected you, it is true, okay. And I have been humbled for it, you see. But now I fear you disrespect me. I want to start over, wipe the slate clean as they say. The only way to do that is for us to be absolutely honest with each other from this point forward. I know who you work for. I want to be sure you are reciprocating my honesty. I want to hear you say it."

"Fine," I say, my face blank. "I work for clandestine services within the U.S. government. If you want me to get more specific than that, we're gonna be sitting here a long time. I haven't asked and they haven't told me. It's an arrangement of convenience and antipathy. But they pay on time, they keep me out of jail, and I have no conflict with any assignment I've been given."

Aiza smiles as the owner of the tapas bar, Paco, approaches with a bottle of Spanish red. He and Aiza talk warmly in their language for a bit and then Paco fills our glasses with healthy pours. Paco takes in the wounds on my face, frowns, and moves away.

"His grandfather opened this place before the civil war," Aiza says, then takes up his glass of wine and gulps heartily. He's ready to open up, the truth I shared like a password to a computer file. "Okay, okay. If I give you my file on Castillo, we both know if you are unsuccessful, it is my neck in the guillotine."

"What did you see today?" I ask him. He bobs his head like he's weighing both sides of a scale.

"I think you can do this, okay. I think of all the bad men I've encountered in this world, you may be the only one who is Castillo's equal. Now I could attempt to play both sides and align myself with the winner when the dust settles and the blood is on the floor, but where is the sport in that? No, okay, I will back you, Columbus. If you go down, then so do I. My die is cast alongside yours. So be it."

He finishes his wine in the next gulp as if to signal the signature on a contract.

He's too dramatic for a fence. I'm beginning to see why Risina despises him. Everything is speeches and wild hand gestures and words, words, words. I'm not sure he even hears himself. His theatrics while prancing around the toy-making woodshop are probably why we're sitting here now and Miguel and whatever the other one's name was are dead. He should've clipped me instead of flapping his gums.

"Can I have the file and get on with it?"

Aiza measures me and then looks toward the kitchen and snaps his fingers. A young boy, no older than ten, jerks to attention, disappears into a back room, reappears a few seconds later, and bounds over to us, carrying a leather satchel. Aiza hands him a couple of euros, takes the satchel, and from it withdraws two folders. The first he slides over to me. Theatrical. Dramatic.

"The folder in your hands contains everything I know about Castillo. Now you hold it and that's that. It's a betrayal of my employment partner, but I have come to terms with it. When it is done, I will either be free of him or dead."

He looks to see if I'm treating this colloquy with the same reverence with which he delivers his half of it, but I just pick up some ham and melon and pop it in my mouth. Aiza grimaces.

"This other folder, Columbus, this other folder contains everything I know about you."

The cover of the folder is bright red. It looks thin, but even one page could haunt me. He keeps his eyes on mine. Is he bluffing? What could he possibly have learned about me?

"You knock out Castillo, you bring me proof, and I'll hand over this file. Any secrets it contains will be yours, okay? Maybe it will protect you. Whatever you get from it, it will be yours to decide what to do. But if you don't kill Castillo, and he comes to me, looking for revenge, this is what I give *him*, okay? And I will feel no shame in it because we understand each other today."

"I don't need further incentive."

"Well, now you have it regardless."

"I could just take it from you now."

"Could you?" he asks, but doesn't look at me, just spoons up a dollop of custard, pops it in his mouth, and licks the spoon.

CHAPTER

5

RISINA'S PHONE SLIPS TO VOICEMAIL AND I LEAVE A three-word message. Her recorded voice hits my heart. I just want to finish this and be done with it and have her back in my arms and Pooley clinging to my leg saying "wanna play with me, Daddy?"

This assignment has me off-balance, like a man coming out of a long, Ambien-aided slumber. I'm wobbly, sluggish, moving through rooms with weights tied to my feet.

Risina. Pooley.

Is it that my assignment, my mission is to kill another killer? Is it that to do so will be assassinating a younger me, a piece of myself, a part of the main? Donne wrote a sermon about not sending to know for whom the bell tolls, so why do I insist on doing just that?

But you see what I'm doing. I'm sure of it. You see how I layer in a phone call to my wife. How I make you relate to me. How I humanize myself.

How I present to you the image of a man swept up against something bigger, a man trying to finish his job so he can return home to his family, to hold them again.

Has your heart gone out to me? Did I cloak myself in just enough truth that you believe the lies? Ask yourself. Do you want the truth? Do you want the ending that makes you shudder? Or do you want the one that gives you warmth? Which will I give you, and which will you believe?

In my experience, people choose the lie every time.

So please, take the lie. I'm begging you.

Risina. Pooley.

Bubbles rise to the surface.

And now, to open Aiza's file, and see if Castillo has a Risina or a Pooley of his own.

Castillo is from a port town named Pasaia in northern Spain, not far from San Sebastian. Mother, unknown. Father, unknown. Real name, unknown. Siblings, unknown.

According to the file, Aiza made a half-hearted attempt to flesh out Castillo's biography after the two of them became assassin and fence. Half-hearted meant he traveled to Pasaia, ate some fish, sat on the beach, asked a few people a few questions, and came back bloated and empty-handed. What he recorded in the file is their history together, and in those details I hope to find the path to Castillo's demise.

The first kill is always the most personal. If a revealing particular is to be found, it will be somewhere inside that first assignment. My initiation into the killing life was a foster parent named Mr. Cox in an abandoned warehouse belonging to the Columbus Textile Company. If someone knew the details of that kill, they could track backward to my real name, my real history, and certainly use that as the first piece of the puzzle to find me. But the people who know about that kill have long since met their maker, and if there was a file that mentioned it, other than the document I wrote to you last decade, it disappeared a long time ago.

How much killing Castillo did prior to Aiza entering his life is unrecorded and will remain in my blind spot. Aiza writes that Castillo was a referral from another contract killer on his roster, a Spaniard named Christopher Ochoa. This is not unusual. I was recruited by a hit man named Hap Blowenfeld at a beer distribution center near Boston.

Aiza figures Castillo's age at the time of their contact to be around nineteen. This was seven years ago. Ochoa had been with Aiza for nineteen years prior to that, and by all accounts was a low-end gunman, more shotgun than sniper rifle. Instead of international politicians or well-guarded corporate executives, or unsuspecting scientists, Ochoa was employed to kill cheating husbands or old matriarchs who refused to die, thus keeping impatient heirs from getting their grubby fingers on an inheritance. It was mean work, rough and inelegant. Amateur ball. How did Ochoa survive so long in the game, doing such low work? Well, he did and he didn't.

Out of those nineteen years, Ochoa spent half of them incarcerated, either jail or national prison. I'd love to tell you I'm an expert in Spain's penal system, but I've had no reason to conduct due diligence. Anecdotally, I've heard hard time is very hard time, and only bribes or serious ransom can reduce a judge's sentence. All this is to say that Ochoa, Castillo's recruiter, was a man of limited skills and limited assets.

After he was brought into the fold, Castillo's first assignment was to tag-team with Ochoa. Again, this isn't unusual. It's an apprenticeship for new hit men, a chance for him or her to learn the ropes, evaluate how someone else does the job. They—well one of them—killed a philandering machinist in Pamplona. The fee was fifteen hundred euros. Low end, low stakes. Aiza barely makes mention of it in the file. Job assigned, job completed, payment collected. No mention of any law-enforcement issues or names in the papers or anything extraordinary.

The second job was the snuffing of a prostitute named Isabel in Barcelona. Ochoa was caught in the act, convicted of murder, and landed in prison. Castillo was neither sought nor arrested for the crime. From then on, he worked alone.

My phone rings and Risina's voice fills my ear. After the *I love you*'s and one story about Pooley and a pile of leaves, I catch her up on everything.

"So Ochoa then," she says, and I can hear just the smallest tinge of jealousy in her voice, like she wants to be doing what I'm doing, this part, the analyzing of the documents and the hunt for the details unwritten.

"Yeah."

"Maybe I should come there for a week," but she says this resigned to the answer she knows is coming.

"That's okay. I have it."

When she doesn't put up a fight, I know I am right about her apathy. Instead, she offers, "Well, at least send me scans of all the documents Aiza gave you. I can look them over while you sleep."

"Okay, I'll find a place to send you a secure wire."

"That's my job. I'll text you the address in half an hour."

"Yes, good."

"If Ochoa brought him in, he knows more than Aiza has given us."

"Yes."

"So why did Aiza not get Ochoa to give him Castillo's history?"

"Good question."

"I don't like it," she says. Her voice is husky when she senses danger, like a wolf's growl.

"You ready for me to start taking the easy ones, the old ladies with the signed wills and one foot in the grave?"

"What would you think of me if I said yes?"

"I'd think you finally came to your senses."

"I don't know. Before Pooley, this was different. Now . . ."

We sit for a long time listening to each other's breath. Neither wants to say it and we both want to say it. I'm not sure how long we remain connected.

Time is a metronome with a sticky pendulum.

Aiza puts me on Ochoa's six but offers no editorial when I make the request. He knows the route I'm taking. If he wondered before, he has his answer. I have to trust that it's in Aiza's best interest not to tip Castillo off. I suppose he could get cold feet and try to walk me into another ambush, but he's seen firsthand the house at the end of that hill.

Ochoa is in Barcelona, so I take the three-hour high-speed AVE train from Madrid Atocha. A wheels-up, wheels-down plane ride would've been quicker, but then I'd have to deal with new guns and I want a chance to rest.

I read a story about bullet train drivers, that the job consists of exactly two actions, taking the train up to speed, and then pressing a foot pedal at least once every two minutes so they know back at the station you're alive. If the driver has a heart attack, someone in the main office can lower the speed remotely. The same article mentioned that a large percentage of drivers with at least a year of experience have witnessed a suicide, someone taking a header off a bridge right into a machine running at 220 kilometers an hour. A cinematic way to go, I guess.

The car is half-full and most of the riders spend the duration of the trip with screens glowing in their faces: phones, tablets, laptops. Two men on the other side of the aisle talk about a robbery in Valencia. A painting stolen out of a church, from what I can make out. "Devils," one of them says.

I think about that bright red folder, the one Aiza held up as a threat, the one containing information about me. He was casual about it, unguarded. If I'd snatched it out of his hand, he would have just smiled at me and said he had another copy. If I'd opened it, it might have been empty. Based on his Castillo file, it was probably just half-baked slivers of information, if anything at all. So why am I thinking about it at all?

In Barcelona, I walk to an address on the Carrer de Casp, a mixed martial arts gym close enough to the sea, I can smell the salt in the air. Ochoa is a regular here, according to Aiza.

I enter El Club de la Lucha, a long name for a small space. The saline air is replaced by the stale sweat of what must be decades of fighters passing through this concrete box, from a time before mixed martial arts put a chokehold on the sweet science. About a half-dozen guys are inside when I arrive, a couple peppering speed bags, four more working takedowns on pull mats. None of them are Ochoa.

"Here to train?" a voice asks behind me.

"Thinking about it," I say.

"Italian?" he asks and I nod. My accent is such that Europeans think I'm Italian and Italians think I'm American. I turn and take in my inquisitor, a fair-haired, orange-skinned man with a boneless nose and cauliflower ear. He probably weighs one-fifty, clothes included. A welterweight. "Five euros for the day or thirty euros a month."

"You got showers? Lockers?"

"*Si, si.* You want a locker? Five euros a month. You bring your own lock."

"Show me."

We walk around the ring in the tight space between the wall and the mats and duck inside a small back room, one shower, one toilet, a pisser, and about a dozen metal lockers, eight of which have locks on them. The shower is on; water sprays behind a plastic curtain.

"Okay, *gracias*," I tell the man and he shrugs as if to say no skin off his nose if I stay or go.

As I leave, the water from the shower shuts off.

Two doors down from the boxing gym is a bicycle shop so I wait there to see if Ochoa shows up today. Aiza said he is in Barcelona, awaiting his next gig, and though he didn't have an address for him, he swore up and down Ochoa worked out daily at this gym, and in fact, that's where they would meet when there were names or cash to be exchanged. So if I—

Ochoa walks out of the front doors wearing a sleeveless shirt and a scowl. He must've been the guy in the shower because he didn't come in under my nose. He's bigger than I thought, at least six-two, and it looks like his body is forged out of iron. He appears to be fit and nasty.

I follow him to a juicery where he orders a blended concoction that arrives the color of grass. He drinks it down and tosses the cup into a wire trashcan on the street, then pulls his phone out and starts thumbing it. The grimace has not left his face and as I move closer, he seems to grow even more mountainous.

"Some place we can talk privately?" I ask his back from about ten feet away.

He slowly lowers the phone and turns the upper half of his torso toward me, like he doesn't want to commit his whole form if he doesn't have to. He flexes his biceps and triceps and lats and neck muscles and I'm reminded of a peacock spreading its feathers, making itself larger, over-compensating.

"Fuck off," he says.

"I found you through Aiza, you dumb gorilla, so you want to go somewhere private to talk or do you want to have this conversation out on the street?" I've learned it's best to talk to people in their language if you want to be heard.

He swivels his whole body now to face me, and I can see the uncertainty in his eyes, so I tell him as much. "I can see the uncertainty in your eyes so let me try to save us some time. I'm not here to kill you. I don't even mean to do you harm. I just gotta talk about a mutual acquaintance of ours. You do so, I'll give you ten thousand euros and you can buy yourself something nice. Or you can bow up and we can meet again at a place where I won't be so generous and we'll talk then under much, much different circumstances."

I can see the wheels turning for him as easily as if he had a forehead made of glass. His shoulders go slack and he grunts *fuck it* and walks toward a coffee shop across the street.

"What's your name?" he asks over the top of a bottle of water. "Columbus."

He raises his eyebrows. "I know you. I mean, I know the name. You hit Coulfret in Paris. The crime boss. Hit him in his own home."

"Did I?"

Ochoa smiles. He's missing the incisor on the left side of his mouth but I have to admit, there's something winning about the smile. "How'd you do that one, brother? I heard he was holed up with two hundred men."

I take a sip of my espresso. "I knocked on his door and asked him if he'd like to make a donation for homeless kids."

Ochoa's smile grows wider and he bobs his head like a puppy that just had a pat. "You. You have a good game. I like it. You don't look like a killer but I can see you're a scary man."

I didn't think Ochoa could string that many words together in a sentence. There's a wisdom in his eyes incongruous with his size. He's growing on me by the second, don't ask me why. There is something strangely amiable about this hulking convict.

"Anyway, some people look scary like me, but sometimes people scare you with their presence or essence or whatever is the word and that is you, Columbus. You have more face than back. Do you know this expression? It means you have a lot of cheek? See?"

"Castillo," I say, shifting gears.

He points an index finger the size of a bratwurst at me. "I knew it. I knew you would say that name."

"Yeah, why's that?"

"What I said about presence. He has the same as you. Only maybe I think he had it born into him and maybe with you, you have practiced it until it stuck if that makes sense. I don't know, though. I haven't known you long enough."

"I understand you brought him into the game."

"That is true, Columbus."

"How'd you find him?"

"Ah, yes. This is how I earn the ten thousand euros, yes?"

"Yes."

"You're going to hunt him?"

"I'm going to kill him."

I watch Ochoa's expression to see if I can read how he feels about this, but as if he anticipated my analysis, he says, "Is good. Is a good thing. I hope you can do it."

"I'm going to do it," I reply.

"Yes, yes. Don't get twisted up about it. I just think he's a dark demon and I won't shed a tear when he's left this Earth so I'm on your side and wish you a good clean hit."

He raises his bottle like he's finishing a toast and drinks to my health. I like that he's a talker. So few contract killers are. I have little regard for men like Ochoa who do this job at a low level, but dammit, there's an infectious twinkle in his eye.

"So give me the details then. How'd you find him? What do you know about him? Try not to leave anything out."

"Why would I?" he answers, his voice throaty and resonant. "I remember it like it was yesterday. But you're going to need to refill your espresso cup and maybe order a pastry or two because this is going to take a while."

My mark was a bricklayer named Edmond Espinoa. I was supposed to murder him in a week's time and get paid something like two thousand euros which I don't have to tell you was a lot of money at the time. Still is, who am I kidding? Which is why when you mentioned ten thousand for me to open my throat I don't mind saying I spent that money in my mind before I gave it a second thought. Money and me, we've never been friends, I should say. I like it, don't get me wrong, but it is always leaving me without saying good-bye. So that two thousand was looking good to me, yes? Like maybe I could trip on over to Ibiza and see a friend of mine who has the tightest bikini on the whole stinking island but that's a story for another time, Columbus. Another time.

Anyway, the money sounded good, and I have no problem killing a man. I never have. Don't ask me why because I cannot say. It just is. Sometimes at night when I'm having trouble sleeping, you know what I do? I count the faces of the men I've killed, the way children count sheep, you know? And it puts me right to sleep. Isn't that strange? I wonder if that's just me or if that happens to other killers, that the idea of being haunted by ghosts is the opposite of what happens. That the ghosts comfort us? I see you're looking at me now with impatience so I will get on with it. But Columbus, you'll have to indulge your new friend Christopher Ochoa. I've never had anyone to talk to about any of this. Fine, fine. I don't want you to think I'm short of lights, yes? That's a Spanish expression but you get the meaning.

So Edmond Espinoa. Aiza gives me a document with all sorts of information and I don't know about you, I mean I'm sure these files are meaningful to you, but to me they remind me of classrooms and homework and nuns with their rulers, yes? So I just get the address of the man I'm to kill and I decide I'll go check him out and get a feel for his routines and maybe I can spot a good place to shoot him in the back of the head, somewhere without a lot of people around, right? At this point, I've already been in prison in Jaen for a three-year clip and I am not eager to go back, no sir. That place is made of devils. Truth.

So I find Espinoa eating seafood at a restaurant where they put the wooden picnic tables outside, and he's got a woman with him and I wonder if this is a jilted-lover killing or an angry-wife killing. Which forbidden fruit is he picking here, right? Do you do that, Columbus? Do you speculate about why you're killing whoever you're killing? Aiza told me when I first started not to worry about things like that but I still do it. Sometimes I go out of my way to find out, even. I know I'm not the smartest at doing this job but I've killed seventeen men and one woman and I've only been caught twice but the second story is coming if you can give me your patience. Don't look at me like that.

I walked up to the seafood counter and ordered some fish soup because it smelled good. I had been to this counter before. It is called La Pardeta and they have excellent mussels. Have you been? Doesn't matter. If you get a chance you should—okay, okay.

I get my bowl and move to their table and sit at the other end and pull out this paperback book I read sometimes while I'm watching people. It's the same book I've had for twenty years and I don't really read it, I just look at the pages while I'm observing. Isn't that funny? That I've never read the book? It's the truth.

So this man Espinoa is bragging to the woman about his football abilities and how it's only because he was in the army he missed out playing for Barca and she's pretending to believe him but it's clear she's heard this asshole's glory story five million times before and when she turns her head to look out over the street, I see bruises under her eye and on her cheek, here and here.

Ahh, so that's it, yes. This son-of-a-bitch is coming home from work and giving his lady a one-two and instead of leaving she decides to take care of her problems through Aiza. Okay. I've seen it before and that's fine. I have my answer.

I let him finish his soup and they canoodle a little bit on the street so he can piss on his tree, yes? And he pats her on the tushy and sends her on her way and they go in different directions. I follow him and think maybe I'll just go ahead and execute him now if he takes a turn up an alley because why wait, you know, I'm not getting paid by the hour, you understand. Don't look at me like that, Columbus. I can see the judgment in your eyes but I'm telling you the facts, so what if your new friend Ochoa isn't an A+ student? I have eighteen notches on the handle of my gun against two arrests for the police and eighteen to two is a victory for any team, yes?

So he walks down a street, don't ask which one, I don't remember, and there isn't a soul out on the sidewalk because if I recollect correctly there was a Champion's League game that night and perhaps Edmond Espinoa is not a football fan after all. Well, bad for him and good for me. I have my gun in my pocket and I'm going to do a quick pass and bang, yes, approach quickly from behind and pull the trigger and be on my merry way.

And I've committed to this, I've increased my pace and I'll catch him before the next block and I'm already looking up at the windows across the street to see if some old crone is watching the block instead of her television, but I'll tell you the truth, Columbus, I was going to shoot him anyway, even if I saw a face in a window because I never really care about the aftermath. I've gotten away with every murder except for two, even looking like me, as big as I am. You know why? Of course you do, but I'll tell you anyway. The police look to motive but the last motive they look for is I got paid to do this, yes? That does not fit into the manual they receive at detective school. Crime of passion, crime of money, crime of rage . . . these make sense. A contract killer? They never encounter one in their entire careers so why should they think of it?

Okay, okay, back to this story. Forgive me, but I have to laugh some-times at what passes for law enforcement in this country. So, I'm walking with a hot gun in my hand, closing in on Espinoa, he's about ten seconds from seeing his own brains on the sidewalk in front of him, and then he turns into a Casa de Emapanes and moves inside. You call them pawnshops, I believe. A pawnshop. Well, here we go, I want to see what this is about, so

I wait ten minutes and I walk inside. The store is of course empty except for the shop owner and Espinoa and now me and they look at me when the door jingles so I pretend to be interested in an acoustic guitar hanging in the window. I *was* interested in it actually. Do you play, Columbus? I have a little talent but my fingers are too fat and slow so I will never be anything but a plucker. Okay, okay, okay. Can a man tell a story the way he wants to tell it? I can see you're enjoying this . . . don't try to pretend otherwise. Ah!

So there's a little television on in the corner playing the football match and I can see this shop owner is impatient to get back to the game and here is Espinoa, haggling with him over a swap he wants, a ring for a fishing pole. I know nothing about the prices of either rings or fishing poles, but from the gist of it, the fishing pole is fancy with a certain reel that can handle a large amount of tension and Espinoa wants a straight-up swap but the owner wants another hundred euros. Indeed, this must be a nice fishing pole.

But now I understand how smart Espinoa is, you see? He knows the pawn-shop owner is eager to get back to the football match, and indeed the owner is keeping one eye on the television and his impatience is obvious and Espinoa wins the battle, gets him to take the ring for the fishing pole and he looks very smug and satisfied as he moves out the door with his bounty. Well, I was going to kill him but I saw the success he had and this acoustic guitar was a very nice one, a Taylor 12-string, yes, so maybe I would get a bargain here too! There was still forty minutes left in the match! But then I thought better of it and also because I only had about thirty euros in my pocket and I suppose I could've pawned the pistol I was carrying but that would've been foolish, I know, and so the door jingled again as I got the hell out of there to resume my surveillance of Espinoa, as he was a couple of blocks ahead of me by now.

Before I caught up to him again, he was on a residential street and there was this teenage boy sitting by himself out on a stoop looking for-lorn, picking up pebbles and tossing them out to the pavement and I was a block away and across the street but I could see him look up as Espinoa approached and I couldn't hear what he said but Espinoa perched next to him and handed him the fishing pole and the boy's face lit up, I mean *lit up*, so maybe it was the kid's birthday or something and Espinoa was showing him the features of this particular rod and reel and it was very paternal or maybe avuncular, I didn't know their relationship but whatever it was, it was this sort of sweet tableau, and I wasn't going to interrupt it by blowing this man's face off in front of this happy boy who may or may not have been having a birthday. I mean I don't know about you but I had very few happy moments as a teenage boy so maybe I have a soft heart because I was not going to spoil this one. At least not until that night and the boy could find out in the morning how hard the world is, yes?

So I decide I'll just break into the house later and kill him in his sleep and maybe toss the place and make it look like a robbery and maybe take some nice stuff to really sell the ruse. Not the fishing pole, of course. And maybe, who knows, I can take the nice stuff to the pawnshop and swap for the Taylor 12-string? Sounds like a plan, yes?

I went to a bar and had a few drinks and a few more and there was a pretty girl there with big eyes so I stayed longer than I should've but she wasn't too interested in me and I looked at the clock and it was one in the morning so toodle-loo to the tequila and I hoofed back the five or six blocks to Espinoa's house. Now, I'm not an absolute moron like I know you're thinking and I do actually care whether or not I get caught so I watch the house for about an hour and make sure everything is still. I'm not exactly new at this.

After my patience wears thin, okay, so half an hour, how am I supposed to wait a full hour, anyway, I approach the front door because you'd be surprised how many people in Spain still leave their front doors unlocked and sure enough, *voila*, it opens. Thank you, you dummy, you just saved me having to pop a window and squeeze my frame through a tight space. I do it when I have to but one time I got a little stuck and that was my first stint in prison—yes, yes, I know that's a story for another time—you need a chance to go to the bathroom, Columbus? Okay, okay. Enough. I hear you.

The door clicks open and there is no dog and no alarm and the place is a little cramped with furniture and knickknacks but not too bad, I mean it looks like a normal entryway, and I notice there's fresh flowers in a pot by the door and that means a woman who cares about things lives in this house. Same woman he was canoodling with? I doubt it. Mother of the boy on the stoop? Ahhh, now we're getting somewhere.

I let my eyes adjust to the light and I'm trying to decide between the stairs or the room to my left when I hear a whimper come from the direction of the room. It sounds human and feminine and even though I should head away from the sound and up the stairs, I move toward it and enter a small living room.

Curled into a ball on the floor is a woman around thirty, not the woman from the restaurant. Okay, so I did look at Aiza's file later and found out this was the wife, the mother of the boy Espinoa had given the fishing rod to, yes, I can see you saw this coming, but in the moment I only saw a woman crumpled on the floor and the right side of her face had been given a savage pummeling. I mean if her jaw wasn't going to be wired shut after that then I don't know anything. I mean it was half sticking out of the side of her face and I could see at least two teeth catching the light on the floor. The woman let out a whimper and whatever primal instinct said to her there's a fresh predator in the room kicks in and her one good eye rolls up at me and she somehow flinches away on the floor. And I hold up my hands as if to say "no, no, no, I'm not here to hurt you," and maybe I whisper it too, I don't remember.

I do tell her I've come to kill the bastard who did this to her and I swear to you she nods at me and in that moment I have my answer. She's the one who hired me. That's clear to me. And I feel good, Columbus. I feel really good. Because some of what we do is soulless work and if we're honest with ourselves it can be a big weight on our shoulders, getting to be the executioner before a judge or jury renders a verdict. Fine, whatever, so be it. There are men who can do the job and don't question it, maybe you're one of those, if so, I tip my non-existent cap to you. But anyway, no matter, I feel good. Because killing Espinoa means he won't do this to any more women, ever again. Maybe that girl he was draped all over at the seafood restaurant, maybe I'm going to change her future too. Maybe she'll never get her jaw broken like this one, maybe she won't be left to bleed on a kitchen floor. So I tell the woman on the ground that I'll be back to give her help, to try and keep quiet, maybe I just put my finger to my lips, you know, all this part is a little jumbled in my mind, but anyway, she nods, I'm sure of the nod, and I leave her there.

I do notice there are a couple of bottles of rum empty on the floor and so I hope that's a good sign that Espinoa is sleeping it off upstairs. I don't know about you, Columbus, I've said it before and I'll say it again, I don't mind shooting a man in the back of the head while he's sleeping. I have little interest in a protracted fight. I mean, if it comes to blows and I have to kill someone with a knife up under his ribs, so be it. But I'm not looking for a fight is what I'm saying. This isn't the American West. If Espinoa is upstairs sawing logs, drunkenly dreaming of breaking women's noses, great. Bang, bang, no more nothing.

I arrive at the stairs, take 'em quietly, they had carpet on them so I didn't have to be too careful, and there were some photographs on the wall of the mom and the fishing-reel kid in much happier times. More of it came clear to me. Espinoa was the stepfather, who knows what happened to the real dad, but Espinoa had moved in on this single mother and turned these happy times represented in the photographs into ones not so happy.

Okay, so I don't want to wake the fishing-reel kid but when I get to the top of the stairs, there are three choices. One door at the end of the hallway, two more the other way. Left or right? There's probably a blueprint of this stupid house back in the file but I told you I don't look at the files. This is much more thrilling for me. You have to use your wits, right? It's the hunt, not the kill, Columbus. It is the hunt for me.

So the door by itself, that has to be the master. I get to it and press my ear against it to see if I can maybe hear any movement or this dumb fuck snoring, something, anything, but it's as quiet as a coffin. Fuck it, I twist the handle and open the door, and I have guessed correctly, it is the master bedroom, but the bed is empty and Espinoa is not there. Dammit, I think. I'm sure I cursed the Virgin Mary under my breath. If this son-of-a-whore went out to another bar . . . but I think to myself, Ochoa, the beat-up woman downstairs would've surely indicated to you he was not home, signaling it somehow. Right? She wants him as dead as you do. So where is he?

The bathroom maybe. Like Elvis, just passed out on the toilet. I love Elvis. Okay, okay.

Well, it wouldn't be the first time I killed a man in his bathroom. It's a good place to do the deed; no one puts up much of a fight when he's shitting. Then I hear a noise back from the other end of the hallway. A scuffle.

Oh, no, I think. He went to molest the fishing-reel kid. I swear that's what went through my mind! So I bound back toward the stairs and one of the doors down the hall explodes open off its hinges like someone shot a cannonball through it and I stop in my tracks. Never have I seen anything like the sight I saw, Columbus. And I've seen a lot of strange things.

Espinoa stumbles out of the room, clutching his neck, and the fishing-reel kid is riding his back like a cowboy, like Espinoa's giving a piggyback, right? And the kid's teeth are gritted and he's pulling something tight against Espinoa's throat, and now I realize it's the fishing line, the line I heard the pawnshop owner say could support a thousand pounds of pressure, and Espinoa's eyes are bulging like a fish pulled into a boat, and his neck is bleeding and he can't get any air so he's just flailing backward and he lurches into one wall and then another, but fishing-reel kid—you see why I call him that now, yes—fishing-reel kid holds on for all he's worth, like a bull rider, he's riding this big ol' nasty bull and I am just watching and I'm sure my jaw is on the floor.

Finally, Espinoa falls to his knees, but fishing-reel kid holds on still, his face feral, his teeth clamped down, his jaw set, and then Espinoa spills the rest of the way forward, his body twitches, and his eyes roll to the back of his head. Dead.

For the first time, I notice the espresso cup I'm holding is empty and I haven't set it down. Ochoa reaches across the table, picks up my half-finished chocolate croissant, tears off a bite, and pops it in his mouth, pleased with himself.

"Castillo's the fishing-reel kid."

"Yes."

"So what'd he do when he saw you standing there?"

"I said 'your mom hired me to kill your dad here, but you already did that.' He said 'he's not my dad.' I said 'my apologies, of course not.' He then asked how much I was getting paid and I told him how much and I could see in his eyes he liked the idea of what I was selling there."

"All this in the hallway?"

"Yes."

"While you're standing over the body of the dead stepfather?"

"Yes."

"And the mother?"

"I helped get her to a hospital."

"You what?"

"What I said, Columbus. I'm not a monster. She was passed out on the floor when we came down the stairs. I helped Castillo get her to a hospital. He wasn't named Castillo yet. She had a broken nose, a broken jaw, a broken eye socket, and four cracked ribs. Why are you looking at me like that?"

"You're not a monster, Ochoa, though you're big enough to be one."

"Well . . ."

"You're actually one of the more interesting people I've met in this line of work. You're either completely honest to a degree I can't comprehend or you're one of the greatest liars born into this world."

Ochoa wipes his hand in front of him like he's wiping words off a fogged mirror. "Nah, I'm not clever enough to sustain a lie, Columbus. I just tell my story to the best of my memory."

"But why?"

"Well, two reasons. One, you offered me ten thousand euros which is about three jobs worth of money for me and like I said, there's a honey in Ibiza."

"That's the two reasons?"

"No, that's one. Those two things I have grouped together. The money and the honey."

"Ah."

"The second reason is Castillo subsequently fucked me."

"Go on."

"You want to hear another story?"

"How much will you charge me?"

"I'll throw this one in free of charge. But you have to buy me another croissant first . . . this one is very good."

Aiza pulled him in and named him Castillo which means "castle" in Spanish but is also the piece in chess that can go up and down and left and right on the chessboard. I've often wondered why everyone else got these cool names from Aiza but for me, I've always just been Christopher Ochoa. Maybe Aiza never thought it would be worth it to give me a false name. To tell you the truth, I like it. Ochoa is a strong name in Spain. I'm fairly sure Columbus is a made-up name, but don't worry, I won't ask. Even if you were about to tell me your real name, I would shout *don't tell me, don't tell me!* I don't want to know, trust me. Where was I?

Oh yes, anyway, Aiza tells Castillo to shadow me for a year or so and learn the tricks of the trade and it's no sweat off my brow because I kind of like the little fucker at this point and feel responsible for him. I mean, in a way I feel like I rescued him even though he killed his stepfather without me and maybe it's my fault for thinking fatherly thoughts. But now I am the knight and he is my squire and he blasts me with about a million questions—how much does it pay, where do you get the names, how does my fence get the names, what's in each file, do I use guns, which type, automatic or sniper rifles, how much time do I have, where do I get the weapons—the questions go on and on, endless and taxing. But I've never had anyone to share this with, this is a lonely profession after all, and so even though I'm annoyed, I'm not *that* annoyed. We do the first hit and it's a good payday and I can see Castillo is hooked. The job went off like a perfect rainbow, all the colors lining up so nicely and I remember Castillo and I went and got steaks for dinner when it was done and I paid for everything. I might have gotten a little tight too, because it was a good kill and the guy was an asshole and I was proud of it.

Castillo was crashing at my house during this time. It occurs to me I didn't tell you his real name. It was Angelo. But Aiza told me to call him Castillo so I did. He spent a lot of time reading newspapers and looking online for any morsel about the death of the prick we assassinated and I tried to tell him that once a job is done, it's done and best to let it go. The inquisitive cuss asked me about a jillion questions about the police too, about homicide, and what I'd say if they came knocking and how to lie successfully to them and I assured him again that the police would never look our way. There was no motive or record of our involvement. That was why we had a fence like Aiza—he protects us from clients and our clients from us. And I was right, of course. There was not even a sniff of a blue uniform near us. A month later and no detectives with notepads ever came to ask us our names or what we were doing on the night of March 25th or any of the things you see on television.

I got the next assignment and it was a piece of garbage but as I've told you, I'm not picky. It was a prostitute in Barcelona named Isabel and I shrugged because whores are easy kills. It is easy to isolate them, it is easy to get them defenseless and vulnerable, and it is easy to get away with it once the hit is finished. She would be my second woman killed and the other one was a lady of the night too. Very easy.

Castillo kept bothering me about the plan, and I told him the plan was to hire Isabel to suck my cock, get her in a motel room, and shoot her in the face as soon as the door was shut. Easy. Simple. He'd come up at me a little bit every day, like a baby bird with its mouth open. *Tell me more of the plan. How do we make sure Isabel comes alone? Which hotel? How do we know which room? What are the entrances and exits? Does the window face the street or the alley? What if we're set up?* It was endless and grating and at this point I'm weary of it, you know? I started calling him Sancho instead of Castillo because I wanted him put in his place a little bit. We have an expression in Spain, "wear the right sized boots," yes? You have this too? Okay, yes, that's it.

Why Sancho? I don't know . . . it is the buffoon who follows around the knight Don Quixote? Yes? So that's what he was. Sancho? Fuck him if he thought I was going to keep calling him Castillo. I'm annoyed and I tell him to stop asking me so many damn questions and if he wants to see me do it, then he can watch tomorrow or he can go back to Pasaia and resume his life as a fisherman. He shuts up and gets real still and I can see a difference in his eyes. It is not unlike when he was choking his stepfather Espinoa with the fishing line, riding his back like a parasite. Same fire in his eyes. Wow, I think to myself. Wow. This boy can sure turn up the dial on his hatred just like that.

The next evening we head down to El Raval. Have you been there recently? It used to be the reddest of red-light districts but has cleaned up over the last ten years. There was a time a man could go there and get anything he wanted for a few pesetas but now the tourism makes you think you're in Disneyland. No matter. There are still areas near the port and Chinatown that have not received the gentrification notice. Yes? So we head down there and Castillo's eyes have cooled and maybe what I said the day before was just a temporary reaction, like a volcano that belches a little steam every so often before falling dormant. I know I'm kidding myself but this is what was going through my mind.

So we go to this cabaret where I know some people, particularly a couple of bouncers, security guards, you know? And I ask about this whore named Isabel, and I have a good description of her, particularly because she has a tattoo of a koi fish on the back of her neck. I never understood people who play dangerous games getting marks that distinguish themselves. But there you have it.

Oh yes, they know Isabel, she'll be over by the Carrer de Pelai probably in the next hour if she doesn't have a trick and this should've been my first hint that all was not what it seemed, because Sancho says to follow him, he knows a shortcut over to the street the bouncer just named. I asked him how he knows shortcuts in Barcelona and he shrugged and mumbled something about walking around when I take naps in the afternoons. News to me, but I wasn't exactly suspicious. I did enjoy my naps and I didn't watch what he was doing, why should I? Maybe that's my problem, Columbus. Maybe I'm too trusting. Like with you. I saw you and I made up my mind, right then, I should tie my boat up to yours, right? I mean, you scared me a little, yes, but I also . . . Yes, yes, okay.

So I follow him around a few streets and my mind is not on anything in particular. I remember it had been raining a lot that week but this evening, the night was clear and even a few stars were brave enough to outshine the lights of Las Ramblas.

There are a few whores up on the block ahead and Sancho struts right up to them and there she is, Isabel, on the corner, koi fish dancing in the water on her neck. The fish's scales were gold but she had embedded some kind of jewel right into the skin of her neck that made the eye glitter. Of course, she had her hair cut short to show off this creation. It was a little entrancing, truth. She was a bit on the thin side but not bad, not bad, kind of attractive for a prostitute. Definitely the hottest of the two I killed.

So Sancho starts negotiating with her and she looks back and forth between us like she's wondering why the kid is doing the talking and what's the relationship here, but her eyes are shiny too, red-rimmed and glossy, and I know she's drunk. All the easier to eat you with, my dear, as the fable goes. Anyway, Sancho is doing the talking and what do I care? The kid is spinning a tale a mile long about how she's gonna be his first and his uncle meaning me has agreed to pay for it because it's his birthday or some bullshit like that. She says "Fine. It'll be one hundred euros" and he says "Bullshit. It'll be twenty" and the way he says it even I wouldn't negotiate further. I mean, he's legitimately scary. You ever seen on youtube one of those jungle videos where the lions are watching the gazelles? That's what he looks like.

So she says "okay" and he takes her hand and leads her to this shit hotel across the street. In retrospect, Columbus, in retrospect, he set this all up. He scouted the area the day before. He knew where she was going to be standing, which hotel to go to . . . he knew which room we were going to get. And this is the part that still gets me angry: what did I do to him? I brought him into this life. I gave him a couch to sleep on. I was willing to show him how to become a killer. And he does this to me?

I'm getting ahead of myself. Just know I've never gotten to ask him why. And maybe that's precisely why I'm helping you now, Columbus. Because it eats at me. Why did the snake bite me? Is it because he's a snake? I'd like to think that. Or did I do something to him? If so, what? Because God help me, I have no idea.

Okay, back to the story. He leads her into the hotel, a word with the ass-hole running the desk, gets a key, and we head up the stairs to the second floor. This place is a real bucket of piss, too. No bother. Better, you know. For the escape. Whatever bad stuff is going on here has been going on a long time and if the police ever cared about this place, they've long since forgotten it. We get to the room and Sancho unlocks it and lets Isabel in and says "just a second," and then he says he can't do it and I say "what're you talking about" and he repeats he can't do it. He doesn't want to watch anymore and he just can't.

I swear to you, Columbus, it was the performance of a lifetime. I *believed* him. Truly believed. And I started thinking, "Oh. This was the thing not in his stepfather's file, you know how there's always something not in the file? Right? This is the thing. His mother, the one I saw cowering on the kitchen floor with the smashed-in face? She was a prostitute. It's why Sancho didn't have a father. It's why she took in that dirtbag Espinoa. She was a former whore. That has to be it! So he has second thoughts about killing this prostitute." Why're you looking at me like that, Columbus? Yes, yes. I go on tangents, I know. It's how I tell things. That's the way it is with your new friend Ochoa. You should be used to it by now, two stories deep. And maybe we'll get to tell many more. I would like to hear some from you. Okay, okay. Back to it.

He says he can't do it and I think I say something smart to him because I'm a little angry with him, punking out at the last moment. So maybe I should've been compassionate but I wasn't and at first, I thought maybe that's why he did what he did, but later, when I had a lot of time to think about it, more time than I wanted if you understand, then I realized, no, Angelo slash Castillo slash Sancho set this all up the day before. He picked the hotel and the room and walked me in like the Pied Piper. So whatever shit he was serving me in the hallway was all a big, fat lie and I believed it like a sucker. He pleaded with his eyes, said he'd stay in the hallway and stand guard if I'd go in and finish it. After that, he'd be done. He'd go back to Pasaia, and he'd be done. "Fine," I said. Fine.

I opened the door and Isabel was already on the bed lying down on her tummy, molted from her underwear, with that fish blinking at me from the back of her neck. And I was unstirred, Columbus. I don't like to drag things out. I don't give my marks last words or last requests or anything cruel like that. I think you have to be a sadist to do that. Someone who does it for the act instead of the job, if that makes sense. That's not me. I only do it for the job.

So I just moved up behind her and took a pillow to muffle the sound and I have a little .38 I use that doesn't pop too much anyway, and I put her to sleep. Not even a lot of blood from what I remember. I guess the pillow or her head being so close to the mattress did it, but what do I know? I'm no surgeon. Anyway, it was done.

I walked quickly to the bathroom just to wash my hands real quick and make sure I didn't have any, you know, of *her* on me and I remember catching a glimpse of my reflection in the mirror and my cheek was trembling. Right here. I couldn't feel it. It just was twitching, I guess. I never noticed this before and I wondered how often it happened. Was this something that occurred when I was under stress? Or did it manifest when I took a life? I was fascinated by it in a sort of detached way, like a doctor coming across a rare symptom in a patient.

I must've stood there for a couple of minutes, just looking at this twitch in my cheek. Then it stopped as suddenly as it started and I thought to myself, "Ochoa, you dumb-dumb, what're you doing in front of this mirror? You better get the hell out of here!" So I didn't even look back at the bed as I passed through the hotel room—what's done is done and I didn't really want to see if the fish was still there or if I'd obliterated its blinking eye. I just didn't. So I turned the knob, ready to escort myself and Sancho out of there, I might've even said "it's done," before I realized the hallway was empty.

I think I'd only been in the room for a couple of minutes at the most. "Okay, well," I thought, "Sancho got the cold feet that ran him back home to Pasaia." So be it. As I'm sure you know, plenty of people have tried this job and found their stomachs turned to mush. There's no shame in that, I guess. I'm sure there are jobs I couldn't do. Cleaning up animals killed in the road? No, thank you. The coroner who opens these bodies to perform autopsies? Blech. I don't even like it when—okay, okay. I swear you have no patience, Columbus.

So where was I?

Sancho split and I'm coming out of dead Isabel's room and I look to the staircase and here come two police officers, emerging into the hallway like something out of a nightmare. And they're not casually approaching, they're coming for me, like they have my description and they have a good idea what I've done. I turn the other way and here come two more police officers, these guys dressed in whatever you call it, riot gear, vests and automatic rifles and Columbus, I just laid down on my stomach and put my hands behind my head and here's the thing. There is no way, absolutely no way they could've gotten there that quickly unless it was all a setup. It's impossible. Not with that gear, not in that tactical position, not in perfect tandem to eliminate any chance of an escape. Two months later I was sentenced to six years in Cáceres.

It would've been more but Aiza got me a good attorney or paid the right bribes or both.

I nod. "Castillo set you up."

"The little prick planned the whole thing. And as I've said, I've never been able to figure out why. What'd he gain from it, you know?"

I shrug. I have an idea, but I'm not going to voice it here.

"So you did your time and you never saw him again?"

"That's right. To be honest, I haven't looked very hard. Some men spend their whole time behind bars plotting revenge against their enemies. Others make peace with God and reach some kind of forgiveness in their hearts. Me, I just ate the time like I was eating a bag of raisins and then looked for him for all of a minute in Pasaia. Now, I don't think too much about the past. It's unhealthy. I like to stay in the present."

I lean back in my chair. Outside, the sun dips and long shadows fall off the furniture in the coffee shop.

"You gonna tell me how to get to him?"

"Columbus, I'm gonna show you myself."

"The mother."

"Ahhh, you pay attention when someone is telling a story. I like that. Yes, the mother is still alive. And for another ten thousand euros, I'm going to introduce you to her."

Ochoa stretches like he doesn't have a care in the world, then pops another bite of pastry into his mouth, wearing a guileless grin. I don't think he knows that his cheek is twitching.

CHAPTER

6

WHICH LIE TO BELIEVE?

I sit on a bench on Carmel Hill, at the park Guell in the main terrace, staring at Gaudi's *El Drac*. What a mind. *El Drac* or "the dragon" is a mosaic salamander sculpture that guards the entrance to the park, a whimsical blue, orange, and yellow tiled lizard. Little piece of broken Spanish tile carefully arranged to make something, original, creative, beautiful. Taken apart, they'd just look like mistakes, jagged irregular pieces of ceramic. But in the hands of an artist, of someone who sees the bigger picture, it becomes a creation.

I'm not averse to keeping company with strange bedfellows. I've done it before, particularly with a young assassin named Ruby Grant whom I might have loved if I hadn't fallen for Risina. If a broken piece of tile has a purpose to serve in a master plan, perhaps Ochoa fits into the mosaic that ends with killing Castillo. If so, I'll gladly use him.

He's not as dumb as he wants me to believe. His vocabulary belies his intelligence. Plus, he's a survivor. He's sloppy, unprofessional, has a methodology antithetical to the way I've done this job for all my adult life, he lacks ambition, and I like him. He's a means to an end, and I like him. He's loud, careless, and stands out like a giant in Lilliput, and, inexplicably, I like him. Risina would caution me about partnering with him, even temporarily, which is why I haven't called Risina today. I like him. I always have been a sucker for a good storyteller.

And yet, the twitching cheek gives me pause.

Or was that a lie too?

We meet at a car park off the AP-2. Ochoa has a grin on his face and holds a small satchel. He has a couple of bags of Tayto chips and some juice. From Europcar, I rented a black BMW sedan for the five-hour drive from Barcelona to Pasaia. We could've taken a train but it's always better to leave a smaller footprint on an anonymous highway.

Ochoa makes short work of the first bag of chips and starts in on his second. I don't mind driving, likely because I feel I have some measure of control.

"I've driven this many times, Columbus. There's a '50s diner in Zaragoza called Tommy Mel's. It is like being in an Elvis movie. Have you been? If we have time, we could stop there maybe? I like it. Maybe you would too. We'll see. Anyway, tell me about yourself, Columbus. We have time to kill. How did you get your start in this business?"

I don't look his way, just keep my eyes on the road. Right when he thinks I'm not going to say anything, I break the silence. "I was raised by my aunt and uncle on a little farm."

"Where's this?"

"Little patch of desert in the middle of nowhere."

"Like Texas or California? I haven't been but I would like to go some day. Especially Texas. I love America. Continue . . ."

"You gonna let me talk or keep interrupting?"

"No, no. Continue. Please."

"One day, we get a couple of new workers out on the farm my uncle pulled in for day labor and I'm supposed to show them the ropes, get them situated."

"Okay, okay. I like this. Go on."

"Well, one of them starts babbling about having to go see a man nearby and the other one is telling him to shut up, and even though they're talking in another language, I get their drift. And so the short one, the one who is spouting off about this crazy old wizard out in the desert—well, I find this video on him and when I push PLAY, it's this cute girl and she's telling the little one to go get the old man's help. He's her only hope . . ."

Ochoa starts to shake his finger at me, smiling. "Oh, you had me, you hateful bastard."

"What?" I say, innocent.

"That's *Star Wars*, you asshole. Luke and R2D2."

"It is? I think you're confused . . ."

"You're a hateful bastard."

"Maybe I'm confused. I thought that happened to me."

"Yeah, keep driving, Columbus, keeper of secrets."

"Fine, fine. The real story."

"I don't trust you."

"No, I'll give you the real story. Are you listening?"

"Yes."

"Okay, I haven't told this to anyone, but I actually grew up in Italy. In Verona, which is where my story takes place. My family, you see, was wealthy and had a huge rivalry with another wealthy family. They had a daughter, the prettiest girl in all of the city—"

"If you say her name was Juliet, I'm going to punch you in the balls."

"Ochoa, I'm trying to tell you about my life."

"Fine, continue."

"Her name was Juliet—"

He throws the second bag of chips at me and I accidentally swerve the car out of my lane, drawing a honk from a passing lorry, but we're both laughing now. "I swear, when you least expect it, I'm hitting you in the balls."

"What? That didn't happen? I get so confused about the past."

"Just drive, Columbus. I can't stand any more lies."

"I can't promise you won't hear any more," I say as I stamp on the accelerator and move around a small Citroën.

In Zaragoza, we stop to get more gas at a service station with only two pumps built out from the corner of a decaying apartment building on the Avenue de Valencia.

"Let's go to Tommy Mel's. It's five minutes away. I'm hungry."

"I'm not going to Tommy Mel's," I reply.

"Come on, Columbus. It's very funny. It looks just like an American diner with the—" and he does a terrible Elvis pose, right here in the gas station.

"What's that?"

"It's Elvis," he says, a little hurt.

"I'm not going to a '50s American diner in Zaragoza."

"Come on, Columbus. It's fun."

"No. If you know an authentic Spanish restaurant near the river, then maybe we can stop. But there's no way, zero, zilch, nada, that I'm going to a shitty, tourist trap, chain Elvis bebop restaurant in Spain. I'm not gonna do it."

Tommy Mel's has a red and blue neon sign above the counter saying "Welcome to the '50s," vintage ads on the walls, waitresses in pink diner dresses, and old vinyl booths.

Ochoa grins from ear to ear and claps his hands together. "Did I tell you? I told you!"

We're led to one of the booths and Ochoa has to fold his massive legs into one of the slots. "Great! This is just great," he says and he means it. I swear he's like being around a big old German shepherd. At first, you're nervous to stand too close to him, but after a while you just want to scratch behind his ears.

Once the cheeseburgers and milkshakes arrive, he starts talking. "Maybe you don't want to talk about your childhood, Columbus, but let me tell about me just a little bit. No jokes this time. I just . . . I told you I don't have anyone to talk with about these things. And maybe it eats at me a little. Tell me now if you're going to make jokes for telling you about my life so I can prepare myself."

I spread my hands as if to say I'm non-committal. I mean, look, I can't promise him I'm not going to make fun of him if he tells a ridiculous life story. I just can't. And as I presumed, my lack of assurance does not slow him down.

"I was always big. Always. People asked me in Grade One if I was in Grade Six. I loomed over every kid my age. People are quick to feel sorry for the small, the weak, but let me tell you, it is not easy being large. Older kids, even smaller ones, take swings at you because of jealousy or curiosity. I don't know but it starts early and it happens often. And you don't have the mental capacity to understand why it's happening, you know, so you blame yourself. I did something wrong. I acted in a way I shouldn't have. I'm talking young, Columbus. Six, seven, eight. And there is nowhere to hide, not with the body I had. The bullseye on my back was visible from across the playground. And the kids my age, they didn't want to stand next to me. It didn't make them feel good. It made them feel inadequate. So I stopped talking. Maybe it's why I talk so much now. For most of my youth, I was as quiet as possible. It was a defense mechanism, like a large fish the same color as the coral, a camouflage, nothing to stand out.

"Teachers thought I was dumb and I let 'em think it. Maybe I was dumb. Maybe I am. But talking in class, out on the playground, on the street, just brought more attention my way. So I kept my mouth shut and when people called me names or tried to start fights, I just pretended not to process what was going on.

"You ever see that movie *Of Mice and Men*? I was George but I pretended to be Lenny. I was the smart one but it was better to be dumb as long as I didn't let anyone shoot me at the end of the movie, right? This act worked for a long time, Columbus. It still does, I guess. 'Cause I'm still the biggest man walking up any street.

"Anyway, to shorten this story, I got a job in protection when I was eighteen for a dancer named Camilla. You wouldn't know her. She had a moment in Spain in the early '90s when she was a big thing and someone at my gym asked me if I was looking for work and next thing I know, I'm one of those big buffoons wearing sunglasses, standing behind the tiny starlet while the cameras pop. I liked the work, the hours sucked, but it was a happy time in my life. There were three of us. Another big guy like me and a third one who was our leader, this little wiry Irishman or Scotsman named Gatins. And he was like you . . . had the look in his eyes that would make men shudder.

"Did I say I was going to make this long story short? Well, now to make it just a little longer. Apparently, Camilla had pissed off the wrong drug dealer because we got ambushed in a back alley sneaking out of a club at three A.M. in San Sebastian. What I remember is two men with guns stepping out into the light from the doorway. What I don't remember is Gatins getting shot in the head, and the other guard, Ram, I guess his name was running away. I don't remember most of it, which still happens to me in a firefight. All I know is once the smoke cleared, Camilla was alive and clinging to my side, and the two shooters were dead, face down on the pavement. One of their arms was destroyed at the shoulder and bent back behind him as though a child had thrown doll parts into a garbage can. The other's face was sunken, as though someone had taken a sledgehammer to it, which I suppose I did with my boot.

"Camilla screamed enough to wake the ocean and the police came soon after. When I was cleared of any wrongdoing, I left Spain for three months. I didn't want anyone from the news or papers or gossip magazines to find me. I just instinctively retreated, the way I had when I was young and the bullies wanted to pick a fight. Then one day Aiza found me at the gym after I returned to Barcelona. I don't even know how he found me or knew who I was or heard about the Camilla incident, but he found me and offered me a job and I've been working for him ever since, except for my occasional time with the government. Can you believe that?"

He said it more like a statement than a question. And I did believe it, for no other reason than my job is to make snap judgments about people who directly affect my life or my assignment. Ochoa is the opposite of me in every way imaginable and yet I feel a pull to him like we're two magnets.

My mother was a whore who never had a chance in this world, born into a hard life with a hard home and yet she was a scrapper. A defiant, determined scrapper. I've often wondered about the nature-versus-nurture question regarding her. If she'd been born into a loving home, with money, into a white family in a Boston suburb, would her trajectory have been completely different? What if she had found a mentor to step into her life? Even at a late age to guide her, to tell her *do it this way, not that way,* to believe in her, would she have ended up somewhere, anywhere besides a Sohio gas station with a knife in her neck?

So maybe instead of drawn to Ochoa like a magnet, maybe that's not quite the right analogy. Maybe it's more like a big brother who sees a bloody lip on his younger sibling, and he's ready to move in and beat the shit out of whoever wronged him, no questions asked. Ochoa might be an entirely different hit man if he'd had Vespucci, or Ryan, or Pooley there to show him the ropes instead of Aiza.

I look over at him, his Brobdingnagian body stuffed into this diner booth.

"What?" he asks.

"You get much guidance on this job?"

"What do you mean?"

"Anyone train you? Aiza?"

"I followed an old man named Toko on my first job. But he was a drunk and a drug addict and he had a crisis of conscience and couldn't pull the trigger but that's a story for another time. You'd get a good laugh out of Toko."

"Here's what I think, Ochoa. I think Castillo set you up with the cops because he didn't respect you. I think he saw the way you approached the job, cavalierly and unprofessionally, and he thought you were blaspheming something sacred."

Ochoa's lip bobs as he chews the inside of it. The fries in his hand hang between the plate and his mouth. His eyes sag, his face draws down. It's kind of sweet actually.

"So why didn't he kill me?"

I shrug. "Some twisted sense of professional courtesy, maybe. You brought him into this game, you were kind to his mother, whatever, so he set you up instead of punching your ticket."

Ochoa shakes his head but he sees it.

"I'm not saying this to point a finger at you or blame the victim, I'm just guessing based on what you told me and what I know about our mark. He's extremely precise, I'm gonna guess narcissistic about what he does, and he thought you were demeaning the profession."

"You think so, Columbus?"

"It's a guess. But here's the thing . . . I don't think you're to blame for the shitty way you approach this job."

"You really know how to make someone feel good."

"I'm gonna tell it like it is, Ochoa. I liked you after I met you, but before that, I'll admit, I understood Castillo's mindset. Anyone who does a job well automatically despises someone who takes it as a lark, disrespects the same work. It diminishes the power and beauty of what we do."

He starts to interrupt but I speak over him. "I'm not saying this to make you feel bad. I'm saying it because I see potential in you that went unrealized because Aiza doesn't give a shit about any measure of standards."

"Ahhh, maybe he does and I am too dumb or lazy to do anything about it."

"You call yourself dumb again and I'm going to put my boot up your ass, I promise you that. Save that bullshit for the bullies in Grade Six. I'm serious."

"Okay, Jesus Christ. I didn't know we were going to get so sober."

"Well, we are. Things are changing for you starting today. I'm going to teach you the right way to do this job and you're going to do exactly what I say, when I say it. This isn't a choice for you. Your free will is gone. You're just going to do it. Understand?"

"Yes, Columbus."

"If this works out, there might be more work for you, making twenty times what you make now."

"Working with you?"

"Maybe."

"Well, that certainly sounds good to me."

"Lesson number one. It's not about the money. This job is never about the money."

"You're the one who brought up money."

I look at him sideways, then take some of his fries and smile. "You're right. Lesson two, forget what I just said about money."

He stares at me incredulously, then starts laughing. I join him, and I have to say, it feels good.

In Pasaia, we hole up in a hotel overlooking the ocean that Risina arranged for us. I only talked to her briefly from the road, and I only reported that I was narrowing in on Castillo, that I had discovered his mother is alive and well and I was going to go see her. I did not mention Ochoa. I don't know why. I am like a man keeping his troubled girlfriend from his parents because he doesn't want to deal with their admonishments. Risina would give me an earful on why fraternizing with other killers is a terrible idea. But I've done it once before as I said, with Ruby Grant, and she saved my life, and then I returned the favor by watching her die in my arms. That one haunts me more than anything I've done pulling the trigger. So maybe this surreptitious alliance with Ochoa is, I don't know, maybe it is some kind of restitution for what happened to Ruby Grant in Siena, Italy.

We sit on a patio with some plastic outdoor furniture and a couple of Don Miguels, and I show him the file Risina prepared on Castillo, or, more specifically, on Aiza. I take him through how I read a file, why each page is important, why there are diamonds in the ore of each paragraph. I explain to him how I pore over all of it, first getting a macro feel before narrowing it down to specifics. I explain why Castillo is unique and why this file is itself unique. That usually a file is a blueprint of a target's life, his history, his movements, his vices, but Risina had failed to locate him within the timeframe the job allowed. I explain how instead she focused on the best way to flush Castillo, by getting to the people who could get to him. Aiza to Ochoa to this moment, right now.

Ochoa absorbs it like a sponge. He doesn't show evidence of a short attention span nor does he mock the bits he doesn't understand. He just takes it in, wide-eyed and curious.

After an hour, he leans back and blows out an exasperated breath. "I never knew. I mean, Aiza gave me files, yes, but nothing like this. Maybe I just didn't know what to do with them. I have to take responsibility."

"No one makes files like my fence, okay, so don't beat yourself up."

"But I never did any of this. I just looked at the name and the address and then stalked the mark for a few days and then pop, pop, done."

"Yeah, well, that's why you were only given these types of jobs."

Ochoa nods. "You ever wonder about who hires you? Like who would want Castillo dead? I told you I like to know with my marks."

I shake my head. "No. I trained myself early on not to care. My first fence taught me something very important that I will try my best to pass on to you. He said that the killer has to make a connection with the target so he can sever the connection."

"I'm afraid I do not understand what that means."

"What it means, what I understand it to mean, is you have to discover something evil, something terrible in the man or woman you're assigned to kill. You find it and you focus on it and you connect with it and you let it consume you. And then, when you cut it out of your life, it's like cutting out the bad part of you, the infection. It allows you to continue to do what we do. So the job is not to figure out who hired you to kill someone, it is to personalize why it is that you, the weapon, are going to kill him."

"Huh," Ochoa grunts. "I never thought anything like that."

"It's how I was taught."

"So what do you hate about Castillo?"

"I'm still working on it. But how he treated you is a start. It's one thing to disrespect someone. It's another to set him up and punish him. In fact, it's downright cowardly."

"Hey, you don't have to tell me."

"Know this. I'm going to hate him before I put a bullet in him."

"I'm already there."

———

Pasaia is a port town with little to recommend it, the brawny uncle to the jeweled princess of San Sebastian. Railroad tracks and sheet-metal warehouses and broken roads, and containers, cranes, and cargo ships. It's industrial and ugly and cast-off. Growing up here would penetrate your soul with desperation, anger, a desire for something more. I know the feeling.

We drive past the port and there are some homes with terraced balconies overlooking the sea, flowers on a cactus. They pass our view in a blink and we're back to the blight of urban planning gone wrong. Ochoa drives, the steering wheel silly in his hands, like a bear with a doughnut. He doesn't seem to mind.

We head inland for a few miles, the streets growing more depressing the farther we get from the water. I wonder if the people here feel like prisoners in Alcatraz, such beauty so close you can almost reach out and touch it, though you're doomed to stay within the confines of your immediate reach. Awful.

We pull up outside a *lavanderia*, not in a strip mall like you might see in the States, but in a blocky cinderblock building on a hill by itself. One window allows us to see inside, and I can make out a few silver industrial-sized machines made in the last century. A couple of dockworkers pass through the front door, having just dropped off duffels of soiled clothes.

"Castillo's mother's name is Angelina Negret. After she picked herself off the kitchen floor, she spent nearly a year in the hospital, undergoing multiple surgeries to her face. The doctors here, they did their best but this isn't the U.S." Ochoa lets my imagination fill in the blanks.

"Anyway, when I got out of jail, I thought about what Castillo had done to me, and I thought I might look for him and get some answers, so I drove here to Pasaia and I went to the house where I saw him strangle Espinoa with the fishing line. But the house had been burned to the ground. I looked for anyone who remembered the family who lived there, but none of the neighbors would talk. I don't know if Castillo—whoever that boy became—scared everyone or maybe just existed in that state where you're there but no one sees you, you know?"

I do know. I've existed in that state a long time. There are ways to hold your body, to avoid eye contact, to dress, to move, that assures you remain in that state. It can be learned, mastered. For Angelo Negret, I'm sure it came naturally, a defense mechanism. The more he blended in, the less he faced his stepfather's fists.

Ochoa wouldn't be able to blend in if he had all year to practice.

"Anyway, I sniffed around for a bit but this town doesn't like strangers. There are plenty of sailors who come and go, but if you linger and ask questions, especially looking like I do, they tend to let you know you're not welcome."

"I've been to many port towns all over the world. They're the same everywhere."

"Yes, well, I was conscious of it and about to let sleeping dogs lie as the English expression goes, and I'd stopped to fill up my car with gasoline when I saw her walking up the street." He points to the front of the lavanderia, where a woman has stepped out to grab a smoke. It's hard to tell how old she is, though she's younger than I would've figured. She must've had Castillo when she was a teenager. She's let her dark, straight hair grow long and half of her face is covered as it spills over her forehead like a veil. But even from here, I can see she's had facial surgery. There are several visible scars from the top of her scalp, down along the cheekbone, and all the way to her chin. The doctors must've done the best with what they had, but like Ochoa surmised, they didn't have the right equipment or were overwhelmed or just weren't talented enough. Maybe a mix of the three. Her face is misshapen, ghastly.

"I knew it was her the moment I saw her. It was as much the way she carried herself as it was the damage to her face. She looked beaten, you know? Withdrawn? So I followed her, tailing her from the car I'd rented, with tinted windows, and she never saw me. I watched for a couple of days, checking to see if maybe her kid would show up, but he didn't. And it wasn't that I didn't have patience that made me give up, Columbus. It was . . . I don't know . . . I started to feel sorry for her, watching her. She had no life. She walked from her home two miles from here, up the hill, sometimes in the rain, and then would come to this laundromat, where she cleaned and folded rough men's clothes all day. I watched her in there, sitting where we're sitting. She has a little station off to the side, where she leans over and folds, folds, folds, all day long, ten hours without stopping. Other than . . ." and he gestures out to where she's finishing her smoke. A few seconds more and she drops the butt and stabs the red end with her toe, then turns and goes back inside.

"And that's it. From what I saw, men don't talk to her longer than they have to, don't even look at her. And I was thinking before this asshole got hold of her, I bet she was pretty. Maybe not cover-of-a-magazine pretty, but attractive, yes?" His voice drops lower, softer. "So I don't know, I just didn't want to watch her anymore. Maybe she and her son are still in contact, maybe not, but I didn't wait around to see. If her life were a movie, I would've turned it off. I couldn't do it."

I look across the road at the sad building and the sad woman inside folding clothes. A tendril of smoke rises from the rubble where she stamped out the cigarette.

"Would she recognize you?" I ask.

⸺

Inside, the light is artificial, stark, generated from a haphazard pattern of fluorescent bulbs strewn about the ceiling. Several silver machines are chugging and gurgling while a few more spin and spin. Angelina looks up when I enter, then quickly looks down. I'm dressed like the dockworkers I saw back in town, or as close as I could arrange in the last few hours. I carry a duffel bag over my shoulder, filled with clothes I bought in a store on the opposite side of town, and then rubbed in the dirt behind the building. It's dark outside now, and from the sign on the door, I know she'll be closing soon.

I move over to her table, sheepish.

"Excuse me, are you the owner?'

She shakes her head.

"Oh, I was curious about getting my clothes cleaned."

She nods her head. "I can help you." She gestures for me to hand her the sack and I do. She weighs it on a nearby scale, then turns back to me. "Eleven euro."

"And when will they be ready?"

She looks up at the clock, frowns. "Tomorrow."

I make that sound of desperation, sucking air through my teeth, like this really puts me in a bad spot. She looks at the clock, then back at me. "Tomorrow is a problem?"

"My ship leaves. I can do it on the boat," and I reach for my clothes.

"No, no," she says, standing up. "Can you wait an hour?"

"I can," I say. "Thank you. And I'll give you fifteen euro."

It's hard to tell, but I think she blushes. I move over and take a seat on the far side of the shop, pull out a newspaper, and begin to read.

After a few minutes, the door opens. Ochoa enters, wearing a scowl. He has to duck under the doorframe to enter, really stoop, and then raise again, the top of his head nearly scraping the ceiling. He gives me only scant notice and then approaches Angelina, menacing.

He asks her a question and she shakes her head. He asks again, louder. Again, her head shakes. The next thing out of his mouth is not a question but a demand. She stands. He grabs her arm and jerks it. She twists away and falls back against the wall. He pushes the desk out of his way as easily as if he were brushing a cloud of gnats. She puts a hand up to shield her face, something she's had practice doing before, in another time, another place. "No," she pleads. "No, no."

And then she sees Ochoa spinning, attempting a wild punch, but I duck it and land two to his stomach. He doubles over and I put everything I can into a hook to his chin. The punch staggers him, and I use his momentum to grab his arm and swing him around and he slips and crashes through the exit door and ends up face down in the parking lot outside.

He made it look authentic.

—⁂—

We sit in a small restaurant by the port that sells plates of meat and rice that look more or less like the pictures in the windows. After Ochoa did a face plant in the parking lot of the lavanderia, I followed and put another kick into his ribs and he got up and gave me a wink to let me know it was all good and then he limped away. He'd told me to hit him, to really hit him, anything less would compromise the ruse, so I didn't hold back. My knuckles are raw but they've seen enough action not to bleed, the way a guitarist builds up the pads of dead skin on his fingers.

Angelina looks like a mouse afraid to come out of her hole. The only movement is her fork, tentatively poking her food. I wear my best smile.

"Are you okay?"

She nods but nothing about the response conveys a yes.

"Do you want me to leave?"

For a moment, she doesn't answer. Then she shakes her head with a gesture so tiny I'm not sure she moved at all.

"What's your name?"

"Angelina."

"I'm Jack. Jack Walker."

"American?"

"Australian."

"Your Spanish is good."

"Adequate."

"No, it's good." She makes the okay sign with her thumb and fore-finger. Her hands are small, her fingers delicate. I wonder if she's passed that physicality on to her son. It occurs to me that Ochoa hasn't described the kid. I've painted a picture in my mind, I always do, and I'm usually surprised by how far off I am, like when I read a book and then they cast the movie and I think *how the hell did they pick that guy?*

"Why'd you help me?"

I shrug. "I don't know. I didn't think. If I would've thought, I wouldn't have done it. It just happened. I saw him hurting you and it just happened."

She takes a bite of meat, leans back, her eyes snapping open like she just remembered something. "Your clothes."

"I'll get them in the morning."

"But your boat."

"I'm the Chief Engineer. They'll wait for me."

She smiles, and though it is lopsided from the old wounds, there is something lovely about it. I can see why Ochoa pulled down his sail and turned ship when he watched her before. There's strength inside this broken woman that softens hard hearts.

"How long have you lived here?" I ask.

"Twenty-five years."

"Married?"

"Who would marry me?" she asks by way of answer and the way she says it is more of a reporter telling the facts than a defeated woman seeking pity. She holds up one of her fingers and wags it. "And don't tell me you don't see me. I despise it when people say that. *Oh, I didn't notice.* I know how I look." And she pushes her hair the rest of the way out of her face so the light finds the damage.

"No, I see it. I noticed. I saw it the first time I looked at you. But the truth is, it doesn't bother me."

"Okay," she says and goes back to picking at her rice.

"When did it happen?" I'm playing the odds not many people have talked to her about this, and most humans want to talk, want to connect with other humans. Make the connection with your mark. But also make the connection with those who can lead you to him.

She looks up, thinking it over. "Seven years."

"Your father?"

She shakes her head.

"Husband? Boyfriend?"

"Husband."

"But you got away from him?"

"Yes."

"Good. I hope he's stinking up a prison cell in Cáceras."

"He's dead."

"Oh," I say. Then tentatively, "Did you—?"

She shakes her head. "I thought about it. For years, I thought about it. And I swore if he ever lifted his hand against my son, I'd do it. With these hands, I'd do it. But I was too afraid."

"It's okay. I was afraid tonight. I understand."

"They tell me my son did it. That my son strangled him while I was unconscious on the floor. But I don't believe them."

"Who?"

"The police."

"Why don't you believe them?"

"Because my son wouldn't do something like that. He was just a boy."

"How old was he?"

"Nineteen."

"Then who did it?"

"I told the police I killed him. But they didn't believe me. I . . . I don't know. But not Angelo. He was sensitive."

"Your son."

"Yes."

"Do you still see him?" I say it as casually as I can muster, interested but still tossed away.

She looks around the room and for the first time, I see a flicker of unease crease her brow.

"I'm sorry. I didn't mean to get personal."

She nods and stirs her rice, burying the pieces of chicken underneath so the bowl is completely white.

"Is there a church nearby I can visit?" I ask, changing the subject to something safe. "If you could point me—"

"I still see him," she says, catching me a bit by surprise. Sometimes when you dangle the worm and leave the cork bobbing, you get a bite.

"That's good. I try to see my mother too," I offer. "It's hard, though. She lives so far away."

"Angelo lives here," she says, and I have to work to hold my mouth still.

———

Ochoa and I sit on double beds in a motel room in nearby Piedra, sharing a bottle of Spanish wine out of red plastic cups. He has a nice purple splotch of raised skin under his right eye from where my knuckles connected.

"You said to make it real."

"But I didn't know you had that in you, Columbus." He's laughing as he says it.

"Then you should have asked."

"One of your lessons?"

"It is. It's like a lawyer with a witness on the stand. Don't ask anything for which you don't already know the answer."

"You have an expression for everything."

"Not everything."

Outside, a couple of headlight beams rake our windows and then a car pulls up outside and the engine shuts off. A door opens and footsteps approach. I watch Ochoa, as his hand moves to the back of his belt and he stands, ear cocked, listening. It's good to see this reaction, a man who can switch his status from idle to alert at the drop of a hat. The footsteps recede and a few doors down, a woman giggles, and a door opens and closes. Just another sailor or dockworker looking to kill time with a woman and a bottle.

Ochoa stretches. His head nearly touches the ceiling. "I'm jumpy," he says, "I didn't think it would be this—"

"Please don't say 'easy.'"

"Imminent."

"Yeah, well, in my position, if fortune's wheel smiles in your direction, you pounce on her."

"So we watch *mamacita*."

"We watch her and we wait and if he makes contact, we latch on to him, and hit him in his sleep or in the shower or wherever he's least prepared. That's how you kill a killer."

Ochoa smiles, his eyes a little shiny. "I like the sound of that." He refills his cup, takes a pull. "But what if she doesn't contact him? What if it takes a month and they only see each other at Christmas?"

"Then we force the issue."

Pop, pop.

We don't have to force the issue.

Three days after I earned Angelina's trust, we follow her up the hill to the laundromat, then back down the hill after the sun drops. Thankfully, the moon is out and though there are no street lamps on this patch of road, we watch her as easily as if she is glowing. Ochoa has done an adequate job at maintaining enthusiasm during surveillance and I teach him a few tricks for fighting off apathy. It's about focus and will power. It's about imagining scenarios before they happen. What if Castillo walks into the lavanderia through the front door? Through the back? What if he appears next to our car? What if he sees us? What if he drives up and picks her up? Over and over again. Imagine every way this might play out and then imagine a few more because life can turn on a dime.

Angelina closes the lavanderia after an uneventful day and we watch her begin the slow march down the hill. If her footprints left marks on the way up, she'd fill them again on the way down, so immutable is her path. Routine, routine, routine. And while my sympathy for her grows, it's tempered by the feeling I always get when it's time to hit the mark: anticipation, excitement.

Tonight is different. When she walks down the hill, she skips the turn that would take her to her house; instead, she walks south, toward the port. I feel that fire in my stomach and Ochoa's breath quickens. He feels it too.

We exit the car and proceed to tail her on foot, a pre-planned catch-and-release method, where one of us follows a few blocks behind while the other rushes ahead and picks her up from the front. Then we flip, which might be difficult if her pace were quick but she's as slow as a yawn.

Near the town center, she veers to her left and then ambles up a small winding cobblestone street for another block, the kind that makes footsteps echo like horse's hooves. I'm adept at masking the

sound but Ochoa might as well be clanging an alarm bell. It doesn't matter, other Pasaians are out and about, the city center is a walking town, most people are on foot, heading to the bars or markets or someplace warm and well-lit for an evening meal.

Angelina has barely looked up; she knows where she's going. Her son's home? I can only hope but the fire that started in my belly warms me all over and I can feel tingles like pinpricks in the back of my neck.

Up ahead, Angelina stops in a doorway and lights a cigarette and I slide into the shadow of an alley. Presumably, Ochoa does the same ahead. As big as he is, I hope he knows at least a few tricks to make himself disappear.

She takes a couple of long drags, then drops the butt in an ashtray pedestal near the doorway and heads inside what appears to be a restaurant. The building has covered its windows with what I'm guessing are rain covers: slats of wood that look like they pull up from slots near the sidewalk and down from the ceiling. The sky is clear, so the owner or manager is too lazy to raise them each night and so makes his establishment more private, I suppose. Maybe that's why Angelina selected it. Or her son did.

After she fails to reappear for a quarter of an hour, I ease from my hiding spot and pass near the restaurant to get a better look at whatever I can and then keep going until I find Ochoa, sticking out of an apartment doorway like a gargoyle. He has his phone out and his face is bathed in a blue glow. "I googled the restaurant," he says.

He flips his screen around so I can see it. A Korean barbecue. The website looks like it hasn't been updated since the dawn of the Internet. No reviews on whatever is the Spanish Yelp. Maybe Yelp. Photos of a couple of dishes but no pictures of the inside of the restaurant.

"We wait?"

"I don't like going into places I don't know; but if he's meeting her in there, I don't want to wait until the next reunion."

"So we go in casual and get a drink or some food—"

"There's nothing casual about you."

"Aww, I can blend in."

I scowl at that one. But I'm itching to change our luck and the truth is, I can smell the opportunity here. She broke her routine and bee-lined straight for this restaurant without looking up at a street sign or checking an address or staring at a map on her phone, which tells me *this* is also a routine, a regular haunt for her, and my guess is she meets her son here. It's private, it's off the beaten path, it's secluded, and he must know it the way I know my own home, all the entrances and exits, all the escapes. Decisions, decisions.

"Okay, we enter five minutes apart and sit near each other at the bar. If there's no bar, we get separate tables. If you see Castillo, you signal me by wiping your left hand through your hair. If I do, I'll do the same.

"Now here's where it gets tricky. She knows my face, which may or may not tip off her son. The moment she recognizes me, acknowledges me, I'll take him out on the spot and you and I will meet each other again at a time of my choosing."

"Okay."

"I'm not as worried about that . . . he doesn't know me and she met me once and barely looked at me. I'll keep my hat low and stay in the shadows as much as possible."

Ochoa nods, he's following. I keep my eye on the door as a couple of Asian sailors exit, arguing loudly in their language.

"Honestly, I'm more worried about you. You attract attention wherever you go. It's your lot in life, I get it, but it doesn't change what is. And he knows your face, so if he spots you, it's going to be quick, it's going to be bloody, and you can't hesitate. You have to be up and shooting and you have to keep firing until he's dead. I'll be shooting too and I won't miss. After, you don't look anyone in the eye and you go out the front. I'll go out the back."

He nods, wipes his face and rolls his shoulders, like a boxer awaiting the opening bell. I don't want to give Ochoa too much time to think about it, so I clap him on the shoulder, say "give me five minutes," and I cross the street, toward the restaurant with the storm-sealed windows.

There are a million reasons why this is a bad idea. I don't know the layout of the restaurant, I don't know how Ochoa will act inside, I don't know how many civilians could get in the way. Too many I-don't-knows, but I force them down because I've learned to rely on instinct and my instinct screams this is happening tonight. Everything building up to Castillo has led to this moment, and it's time to get the job done and get back to my family. If there is an ominous premonition, I don't feel it. Maybe my senses are dulled by worrying about Ochoa or just partnering with him or maybe I projected intelligence on to him when he's just a big, dumb oaf with a gun. Or maybe my altercation with Aiza's men in the wooden toyshop rattled my brain and I'm not thinking clearly. Whatever misgivings I have, I clamp down and enter the door without looking back.

The restaurant is dark and sparsely crowded. A waitress greets me with a perfunctory smile and asks how many in the strangest accented Spanish I've ever heard. I can say this is a first, a matronly Korean woman in a tough Basque town, speaking Spanish as a second language. A pair of dark curtains obscures the view into the larger restaurant, but I can see inside a gap to a small bar so I ask if I can sit there and eat and I'm not sure she understands and I start to grow uneasy because the last thing I want to do is call attention to myself. So I hold up one finger and just say "one," and she repeats "one" louder than I would like and says something I think means "how sad, only one," and if this woman doesn't stop chirping at me I might have to throw a stray her way when the melee starts. There's nothing wrong with the woman, not really, but the evil in me is growing the way it always does in the moments before the action starts.

She takes me to a table near the bar and I sit so my back abuts the wall and I can see into what I hope is the only section of the restaurant where customers enjoy their meals. It's the kind of place with hibachi grills embedded into the table and the customer is supposed to cook his meat. The place smells like fried pork and steak and chicken and a teenage boy approaches and uses a chimney lighter to fire up the grill and pours some oil onto the top of it to get it sizzling.

I'm seated at a table for four but the restaurant is lined with booths and I don't see her. There are a half-dozen other diners I count from my vantage point, but she's not one of them, no one fits her size or her description, so if she's still here and didn't duck our tail, leave out the back, then she's in one of the booths.

He's here. I know it. He's been a killer a long time now, a battle-field veteran, and by every account a damn good one, a Silver Bear in his own right, and so he follows his protocol even when he's doing something as innocent and private as eating a meal with his mother. He selected a booth in the back, farthest from the door, nearest to the kitchen, where a customer would have to explicitly be looking for him in order to wander over and interrupt. I spot steam rising from the booth, so mother and son have already ordered and are beginning to cook their dinner. But dammit, I'm not sure. I have no visual confirmation. It could be anyone. Or she could be alone. I feel like a chess player on my heels facing a superior opponent, powerless to stop the attack. Or maybe I'm just an inferior piece: I'm the knight; he's the rook.

I should just give up, retreat, pick up the game after the pieces are reset. I put my napkin down and am just about to stand when Ochoa ducks through the curtain into the restaurant, scans the room with the grace of a lighthouse beam sweeping over land and sea, and sits at a table diagonal from mine, so I can see the back of his neck.

He does that thing where you use the palms of your hands to stretch your neck but it's a clumsy excuse to look at me, gather in quickly what I know, but I give him a shake of the head and do my best to convey with my eyes that I don't like this setup. The room's too dark, the booths too obscure, steam rises all over the place, pots and pans bang and knock around in the kitchen as loud as a marching band, the strange Spanish by way of Seoul loud and obnoxious and we should fold our tents and get the fuck out of here but it's hard to convey all this with my eyes. Ochoa picks up none of it and orders some chicken and shrimp in a voice too loud for the room. The waiter passes over to me and I just wave him away and pretend to study my menu.

Ochoa has a big bottle of Alhambra beer delivered to his table and it is soon replaced with another. He turns and looks at me again and I toss a nod toward the corner booth and he nods back in agreement. Well, yippidee doo, at least we have that.

I don't like our position relative to the booth. If Castillo emerges, he can take both of us in with one look, but we're committed at this point so we might as well let whatever happens happen. I check over my shoulder and it looks like I have about ten feet to the kitchen door if I need to tag out. To the left is the bathroom door. If there's a window or a way out there, it is unknown to me.

A waiter appears next to Ochoa's table with a dozen bowls of sauces and vegetables and uncooked meat. He then comes to me and asks a series of questions so I nod and point at the food on Ochoa's table and he smiles and does what I really want him to do, leave.

The waiter heads from my table to the booth we have under surveillance and as he reaches for a water glass, I see a feminine hand reach out to let him refill it and at least I know she's here, exactly where I thought she was, and Ochoa turns to me and raises his eyebrows, he saw it too, a hint of a smile because our joint instincts are valid.

Ochoa has one hand under the table and I know his gun is there, ready. One couple has left, so that puts collateral damage at four other diners, four waiters, a hostess, and only a few cooks in the kitchen.

Food arrives by way of the dozen bowls and I throw a couple of strips of meat on the grill because I don't want to look conspicuous. My stomach rumbles. How long has it been since I ate? I'm not sure.

Ochoa pops meat in his mouth like it's popcorn, all while his left hand remains under the table. There's a shuffle at the booth in question and Angelina emerges from her seat, presumably to go to the bathroom, and the man sitting with her gets out and stands, a gesture of chivalry that fits in this town like a block of cheese into a keyhole. And he hasn't turned but he's the right size for Castillo and his hair is black but something is off. I don't know how I know but I know. The way he helps Angelina out of the booth; it's so polite, and then I see it. He's wearing a clerical collar. He's her age. This man isn't her son. She's dining with her priest.

Angelina leaves the *padre* with a smile and heads my way, toward the lady's room. I lower my eyes so maybe she won't spot me, but she does, and a look of confusion blooms across her face because I told her I was on a ship heading out to sea and instead I'm here in a Korean barbecue in Pasaia.

Ochoa rises from his chair with his gun up and crosses toward the man at the booth, a bull after a red cape. He must not have seen the clerical collar. He doesn't realize the man is not—

Pop, pop.

Ochoa's head explodes before I have a chance to warn him.

Most men gawk at gore or flee from sudden violence but I am not most men. Trained over a lifetime of making kills and besting those who would put me down, instead, I deduce from the way Ochoa's head caroms forward that his killer is to my right, only a few feet away, and when I turn, Castillo's doing what I would've done, not admiring his shot but sweeping the room for the next threat.

In the blink of an eye I take in the following: Castillo looks younger than his years and most likely uses this attribute to his advantage. He has a baby face, no wrinkles, no facial hair, wide eyes, brown, and is therefore subconsciously, aggressively, unthreatening. He has two automatic handguns; both look like Glocks but I can't tell.

His eyes travel from his mother's to mine and those guns turn my way. I'm not going to have time to get my weapon up so I lunge out of my chair, plant one foot on the ground, duck his arm that swings my way and tackle him with everything I have on to the nearest table.

He flails back and the only luck I have going for me is he's surprised. Maybe he was late in joining his mother and her priest for dinner, maybe he was just watching his mother to see if anyone was following her, hanging back the way assassins do, but at some point he spotted his old friend Ochoa entering the restaurant, the one he sent up the river, the one he wasn't going to give a chance to explain himself, and *pop, pop,* Ochoa is gone. He didn't see me, though, didn't realize we were working this as a tandem hit, or one of those two gunshots would've been aimed at my head.

I have Castillo off-balance but not for long. I have my hands on his elbows so he can't get those guns around on me, and his back is to the table, but the tabletop is not lit and that gives me an idea.

I crane my neck and see steam rise on the table Ochoa vacated, the pork or steak he was cooking still sizzles, and with all my strength I drop my hands from Castillo's elbows, grab his jacket in my fists, flip my weight and swing like a shot putter.

We roll into a 360 and I pirouette right on top of Ochoa's table. Castillo screams as I pin his arms to the hibachi grill built into the tabletop and it sears the backs of his hands. He drops his guns out of pain and drives his forehead into my stomach which I've left unprotected.

This is one of those fights. We aren't here to question each other or shame each other or glean information from each other. This is a fight to the death and when those fights happen, all bets are off. No one quits, no one gloats, and no one tires until brains are on the floor.

I spill backwards and he's on me and our positions reverse as I fall onto my table and the back of my head collides with the grill there which is lit and hard as a rock and the pain is immediate and deafening in its power. Castillo climbs on my torso and I can see his teeth, his lips snarling, his eyes murderous, and the back of my head is throbbing and through all that I realize he's not punching me and his hands are going for the Glock in my waistband.

He has it and it's going to be the end, this is the end, this can't be the end, I won't let this be the end, not here in a port town in the north of Spain and not at the hands of this kid.

Before he pulls the trigger, I snap my shoulder into his chin and I feel it rattle and he falls away and I push forward and snap one, two, three hooks into his ribs.

Outside, faint for now, police sirens interrupt the usual boat klaxons as they draw closer. Despite the body blows, Castillo hangs on to my gun. When he tries to raise it, I feign another body shot and he drops his elbows to protect his ribs and instead I hook his chin, hoping to break his baby-faced jaw.

The Glock flies from his grip. The sirens are practically on top of us, and I'm about to make a play for my gun but out of nowhere, Angelina, Castillo's mother, smashes into me like a wildcat. I was so intent on eliminating the nearest threat, I took my eye off the other danger in the room. She attacks like she's possessed, and nothing I've witnessed in her over the last few days hinted at this level of strength and swiftness.

My sympathy for her is gone in an instant and I smash one fist into her stomach and the next into her temple and she topples like a brick wall meeting a wrecking ball and when I scramble to my gun and look up, Castillo is gone.

Not there.

Not where I'd left him.

He'd used her attacking me as a distraction to escape out the back door.

He'd left her behind. If I killed her, so be it.

The sirens are right outside.

CHAPTER

7

I'M ON THE HIGHWAY BACK TO BARCELONA, MY MIND racing as fast as the car. There are thousands of possibilities of what went wrong, and none of them are pleasant to face. Most disturbing is that Castillo, who must've maintained a relationship with his mother even after he became a contract killer, left her at my mercy to save his own skin. Used her to flee as indiscriminately as if he had tossed a flash-bang grenade. She meant something to him only to a point, and then she became just another chess piece on the board. Sacrifice the queen, and pull back the rook in order to take down the knight another day.

I shop in a service station just long enough to purchase a pre-paid cell phone, what we call a drop phone, and to fill the tank with gas. I don't remember eating so I grab some jerky and some kind of energy bar with a name in Spanish I've never heard before. It tastes like chemicals.

The car smells like Ochoa's chips and Ochoa's drink and Ochoa. Live by the bullet, die by the bullet and all that bullshit, just another poor sap whose life intersected with mine and, soon after, ended. Bad thoughts, push 'em away, strap 'em down, concentrate, Columbus, concentrate. There's a job to do and another way to finish it. There's always another way.

Risina waits until the third cycle of call-and-hang-up before she answers a number she doesn't recognize. The dark men gave us fancy equipment and software to make our calls untraceable, so they said, protected, private, but we prefer our backup system of random drop phones bought at convenience stores.

"Hello," she answers, anxious.

"I don't have good news." I try to keep my tone level, but it's hard to mask disappointment. I tell her everything now, Aiza to Ochoa to Angelina to the shootout in the barbecue in Pasaia. I know she's already on the Internet, reading up on what the police know, what they're reporting. The crime rate is high in that port town, but a gunfight is a gunfight and newshounds sniff the same blood trails all over the world.

"Okay," she says, "so the mother is not an option."

"I could grab her and hold her and he wouldn't give a damn. I'm sure of it."

"Maybe he just wants you to think that so you'll leave her alone."

"He abandoned her to die. Trust me. It wasn't a strategic move. I could've killed her as easily as whistling Yankee Doodle."

"I'll have to hear you do that some time."

I can't help but smile. Risina. No assignment gone sideways will keep her from lightening the mood. "Trust me, I'm good at it. I could lead a symphony with my whistle."

"I'll call and reserve the Met when you get back."

"Good."

"Where are you right now?"

"On the way back to Barcelona."

"Aiza?"

"Yeah. You got a better idea?"

"What're you gonna do once you have him?"

"Negotiate for a meeting."

"Castillo will never go for it."

"No, but he'll know I'm with Aiza. And maybe that will provoke him."

"Ahhh, he'll come looking for you. The spider draws the fly."

"Exactly."

"I love you, little spider."

"Give Pooley hugs."

"You bet I will. And I'll say these are your daddy's arms squeezing you."

I can picture it.

The wooden toyshop is closed and no lights are on in Aiza's apartment. I make quick work of the lock to the shop. It's a single-cylinder deadbolt, surprising for a man with so many secrets but maybe not so surprising for Aiza. The shop looks the same as when I last left it, minus the dead bodies and the blood on the floor. It's as if they were never there and the shop could open this morning, ready to bring joy to children's hearts. Maybe it will.

I pass the area where I dropped the two bodyguards, the same ones who gave me a beating, and the fleeting thought hits me that no one is ever going to tell their stories, how they began, the bad decisions they made, the moment when they took the left path instead of the right and their lives crossed with mine and whatever plans they had, relationships they had, friendships they had, ended, just like that. Or were they writing heroic epics with themselves as the protagonists? Or maybe tragedies charting their falls from grace? Or were they telling lies like I do, forcing their listeners to sympathize with their struggles and misfortunes and decisions so they could somehow be forgiven?

And isn't the truth just a different lie?

On the workbench under the pegboard is a small puppet, a marionette with a long wooden nose, Pinocchio. He's wearing painted German lederhosen and red circle cheeks and a tuft of black hair and he's staring at me, lifeless, his legs and arms spread in inhuman positions, no one to pull the strings, to make him dance. No wishes to ask. Wishless.

I presume, correctly, there is a door with a staircase behind it that leads directly up to Aiza's private apartment. This one is padlocked, which I find funny seeing as there are literally hundreds of tools within easy reach of the lock. Again, quick work and I move upstairs.

My ears are acute to the sounds humans make. We are a noisy species, always tapping and snorting and snoring and coughing and whistling and doing things animals do when they are at the top of the food chain, the things that make it easy for assassins to locate their marks. There are none of those sounds above me. No one is home.

The stairs are wooden, probably made right here in this shop, so I stay light on my feet and stick to the edges to keep creaky boards from creaking, just in case, and open the door into a spacious apartment, decorated more fastidiously than I would have imagined. Couches with fussy pillows and artwork with expensive frames and a fireplace with a custom-built screen to fit its novel dimensions and a bookcase arranged with book titles all facing down. There's a sensitivity about it that suggests an artistic touch.

Empty, empty, and the other rooms in the house: kitchen, two bedrooms, a closet, all empty. Aiza is out on one of his morning excursions, I presume, so I have a choice to make. Sit here and wait for him to return home or go out and try to catch him on the street. I decide on the former, but the pit in my stomach says time might not be on my side.

I know from Risina's overview on Aiza, he does not have an office. When he whistled at the boy at the restaurant and the boy ran over with Castillo's file and also a red one, his file on me, I wondered if it was a bluff, the old "Spanish Prisoners" con where the red folder had nothing in it but shaved newspapers. Maybe Aiza was full of shit. But if that file is real, perhaps it is in this house.

I begin to search the usual hiding spots: floorboards, attics, walls; but an hour later, I have nothing to show for my efforts. I'll have to ask him about it when he returns.

The second sense one acquires when he's been hunting as long as I have kicks in. The one that says things have gone terribly wrong. The one that says retreat, regroup, reevaluate, and start over. The one that is unexplainable and yet as reliable as the sun.

I phone Risina and tell her to book me seats under three different names on three different airlines going three different routes to get me home and she says "yes" and knows better than to ask the usual wife questions: *Why? What's wrong?* Almost as soon as I press the button ending the call, I hear the first police sirens. From my vantage point on the second floor above the wooden toyshop, I spot one cruiser and two motorcycles closing from both directions on the Huertas.

They must be coming for me. Either Aiza owns a more sophisticated alarm system than I gave him credit for, or he spotted me inside his home and phoned it in. The second choice seems unlikely. People in our profession don't call the police.

Back down the steps into the toyshop and I'm expecting the police to smash the door in at any moment, but the sirens stop. Blue lights continue to flash, strobing through the shop's front shade, but still no uniforms storm the building. I hear a crowd gathering in the street, the curious attracted to police lights like moths to flames. The pit in my stomach grows.

I cautiously duck out of the back of the store and check in both directions for signs of tactical maneuvers from the Barcelona police, one team in front, one in back, but nothing, at least not yet. Fine, the alley is empty and there is daylight and still no second team and experience tells me I should walk away, put as much space between Aiza's residence and my feet as I can, head to the airport, retreat, retreat, retreat, but the police and a crowd are gathered in front of the toyshop, in front of Aiza's apartment, as I round the corner from the alley to the street. The reason they are there is tied to all of this and I need to know. It makes sense to know.

I pull my hat low so the brim shields my eyes, button my jacket, and join a group of men who are drawn like carnival-goers to a freak show. We crowd closer, easily a dozen men and women in the group of gawkers with me as one policeman shouts to *keep back, keep back*, and now I see we are gathered around my rental sedan, the one I drove from Pasaia to Barcelona and parked here. The one Risina rented for me from Europcar and no one in Barcelona would possibly know about.

Except. Except if Castillo did not flee the Korean barbecue to head for parts unknown. If, instead, Castillo fled the Korean barbecue to lie in wait, to watch me emerge, and follow me all the way back to Aiza.

This is disturbing. I'm an expert at shaking a tail, both on foot and on the road, and I've always been careful, so if he followed me, well, fuck me . . . who else has a history of calling in anonymous police tips?

Is he watching me now? He must be. *Pop, pop.*

It is imperative to cut bait and get the hell out of here. One of the police officers pops the trunk and the crowd on that side of the car reels backwards. A terrible wave rises in my stomach, my throat, my whole body as I, with the throng of gawkers, move like worshippers around the Holy Wall, a whirlpool of rubberneckers, all wanting to see inside the trunk despite the officers yelling louder, *get back, get back,* and as we circle, I see what has the crowd chirping.

Aiza is in the trunk, well, that's not exactly true. Aiza's head is in the trunk, severed at the neck like he had been put under a guillotine. The police blow whistles now like we're at a soccer match that has turned into a free-for-all and yes, forget this, now is the time to flee, but before I take ten steps, I hear a voice yell louder than a megaphone, "That's him! I saw him! That's him!"

I know, before I turn, the voice is Castillo's, and he's pointing at me.

What I'm not prepared for are two details.

One, he is wearing a police uniform matching the other officers.

And two, he's holding a red folder.

I'm in a fetid cell on the outskirts of Barcelona with a bruised and battered face and I'm futilely and impotently angry. The details of how they chased me and caught me are simple, there were too many of them, coming around corners like a flood breaking through a levee and I made the tactical decision not to kill anyone. I pinned my hopes on two things: that like in the states, they'd give me a phone call; and, more importantly, that Castillo wasn't really a cop, that he'd stolen the uniform.

In the split second I saw him, I took in the details: his pants were too short, the sleeves too long, so he hadn't worn the uniform long, perhaps only today.

I need that phone call. I have to have that phone call, but it has been approximately nine hours since I was arrested and all I've gotten is roughed up in the street by three cops who pinned me down and roughed up in this cell by three different cops who tossed me in. They do not like that I won't open my mouth except to say *telefono*.

Now all I can do is sit and hurt and stew.

If Castillo goes straight to the airport and gets on the first flight to New York and knows exactly where I live, knows about Risina and Pooley, if that information is in the red folder, then at best, at *best* he can be there in thirteen hours. That's what I believe. I'm not going to be generous and presume it will take him longer. I can't. I won't. This job forces you to presume the worst. Best-case scenarios are for dead men and suckers.

Another hour passes and the door down the hall does not open. There is no other sound in this cell except for my breathing, strong and defiant. My pulse beats in my ears and I concentrate on controlling it, slowing it. The difficulty increases with each passing minute.

Somewhere around half an hour later, the heavy door down the hall slides on its guide track and two elephant-sized guards enter.

"Telefono," I say.

The room has soundproof tiles, a wooden desk, and five detectives staring at me, standing or leaning against the wall while the twin giants who brought me in and sat me down loom somewhere over my shoulder. There are no windows or mirrors or one-way glass or video cameras to record our conversation. This is not a good sign.

After the lead detective who introduces himself as Belmonte closes the door, he slowly, deliberately pulls a chair close to my knees, like he's been watching Hollywood films from the '30s. He has the mustache; he's only missing the fedora.

"What's your name?"

"Telefono."

Slap. The guard behind me pops the back of my head, rattling my teeth.

"Your name?" Belmonte asks again.

"Walker. Jack. Jack Walker."

Slap. This time from the other side, the second guard. At least I know it doesn't matter what I say.

"Whose head is in the trunk?"

"I'm going to get slapped but I can honestly tell you I have no idea."

Slap.

"Whose head is in the trunk?"

"I don't know."

Slap.

"Whose head is in the trunk?"

"John the Baptist's," I answer.

Slap.

I've been interrogated many times before, by much rougher men than these beasts behind me. Their hands will break long before my spirit, but time is a goddamn factor, though I can't allow them to know that. There's a giant, round black-and-white clock, the kind you find in schools, hanging on the wall facing me, over the detectives' faces.

I force myself not to look at it. Not even a casual glance. Not even a flick of the eyes.

Detective Belmonte starts to open his mouth again, but I'm quicker.

"Detective, trust me when I say you're not now, nor ever going to get the answers you're looking for. You're never going to know whose head is in that trunk, you're never going to know who I am, what I'm doing in Spain, who the man was who beat up or killed a Barcelona officer today and stole his uniform, why that man pointed his finger at me. You're going to run my fingerprints and no records are going to come from anywhere, ever. You'll run my face through every bit of recognition software you have, checking your own database, Interpol's, the FBI's, CIA's, Mossad's, FSB's, and every other system you can think of, and they'll all say the same thing. Zero.

"I have no identity. And I understand that's gonna eat at you, haunt you, and thirty years from now when you're smoking cigarettes on a beach in San Sebastian, thinking about the job, the old days, this case is going to be the one that sticks in your craw.

"Now, I need a telephone. I've been asking for one since I got here. Not in a week. Not in a day. Not in an hour. I need a telephone now. I'm going to make a call. You can watch me dial the number, you can listen in to the call, you can trace it, untrace it, analyze it, study it until you're blue in the face." I can feel my rage growing. I want to stay calm through this growing speech but I just don't have the energy. "And the sooner you let me make this call, the sooner you will get to go on accepting that you will never, ever know a goddamn thing about me or what happened today."

The five detectives gape at me like aquarium visitors looking through the glass of a shark tank. Above their heads, the clock makes a *thunk* as the minute hand reaches its apex.

Slap.

Another hour passes while they must be debating and making phone calls and waking up bureaucrats. A cut above my eye is open and unchecked blood trickles down into my eyelashes. The guards came around to give me a few more licks after the detectives left the room. I took it until they tired.

The clock continues its loop, malicious and remorseless.

Finally, the door opens and Belmonte sticks his nose in. He looks like he is the one who has been worked over. "Get him up," he says.

A hallway, another room, a second hallway, and then a smaller room to hold me. I hear activity on the other side of the door, tables moving, chairs sliding across the floor, equipment brought in, unboxed, and set up. It's like the ballroom of a hotel as it is readied for a banquet. All the while, *tick, tick, tick*. Creeping up on twelve hours since they tackled me on the Calle Cadiz. Or is it thirteen? I might've lost an hour somewhere.

The guard who pummeled me picks broken skin off his knuckles and then licks the wound, tasting the blood. His or mine, I don't know. There's a part of me that wants to break his nose, the back of my head to the front of his face the next time he stands behind me to uncuff my hands. I cage the thought. Maybe another time, under another circumstance. For now, I ignore him, a strategy I learned a long time ago when dealing with big men. It can be more effective and more maddening than a physical blow.

The door springs open and Belmonte enters, physically nervous, a foreign feeling to men like him. He rubs his nose, rubs it again, tries to smooth out his mustache, but his gestures are just physical manifestations of the inside of his head: uncertainty, helplessness, vexation. You can tell a lot about an adversary by watching his hands.

"Okay, let's do it," he says without looking at me.

I rise, still handcuffed, and follow him into a larger room, dimly lit, crowded with people. Most wear suits bought off racks at discount stores, and if there are indoor anti-smoking laws in Barcelona, they're ignored here. Competing for light with the red tips of cigarettes are dozens of laptop screens, open and operating. Technicians or possibly analysts are interspersed throughout the detectives, ready to record my every inflection.

I'm offered a chair at a desk upon which one item rests, a commercial phone with multiple lines indicated on a panel down the right side. Belmonte presses line 1, hands me the receiver, and asks for the phone number. The technicians and analysts click their computers, soundwave files start to spool across screens. The show begins.

"001-202-441-6913."

Belmonte dutifully punches the numbers into the keypad. The tension rises in the room as if a thermostat is dialed up ten degrees. No one makes a sound as the robotic ring begins. It only rings once.

"Bailey's?" a female voice says.

"O4131769413288175," I say and the line goes dead.

Four seconds of silence follow. Only the amplified dial tone reverberates through the speakers like an electric guitar left humming on a stage after the encore. I lean back in the chair and for the first time since my outburst in the interrogation room, I allow emotion to cross my face: relief.

Then the room erupts, a symphony of colliding voices, computer beeps, and my voice coming out of the speakers again and again, "O4131769413288175."

Belmonte's knees buckle and he sits down in a daze, lucky a chair is there to keep his ass from crashing to the floor.

He was expecting answers and all he got was more questions.

The moon is out, dressed in an autumn yellow and shining in full glory. I am in a better room, still a cell, but this one furnished with a bed, a desk, some books and a private bathroom. There are two guards posted at the door. I don't know why they put me in here, what appears to be some kind of lieutenant's quarters, but I can guess: fear. Fear of the unknown. Fear that they fucked up by roughing me up, arresting me. Fear that I called someone with a lot of power. I haven't used that number nor that code before, so I don't know what to expect, but I hope their fears are realized.

The code I used is one of extreme distress.

The dark men told me it would protect my family, if I ever got in a jam. Perhaps my trust in them is misplaced, but it was the best option I had.

Two days with the company of my enemy: not knowing. I've mentioned him before, the devil who works over your mind like a heavyweight, not knowing. You have to concentrate to ward him off, but not knowing is always there, waiting in the dark, ready to go at you again. He stays in my cell, rides my back, pummels my brain with dirty punches.

Then the doors open and Belmonte steps inside. It's obvious: not knowing has worked him over as well.

"You're, uh, you're free to leave."

I stand up and head straight for the door before anyone can change his mind. Belmonte grabs me by the elbow as I pass. He leans in close to my ear, his breath stale. "Who are you?" he asks, pleading. "Tell me. Please."

"I'm no one," I tell him. "Forget me."

I know he never will.

Lavender waits for me at the front door, wearing a crumpled sports coat and a foul expression. If he expects me to be remorseful for calling and using the code his agency taught me, he can stuff it up his ass. No one at the jail asks to process me out. A door buzzes and opens. That's it.

As soon as we clear a hundred feet from the station, he starts with "what happened?"

"My family?"

"Safe."

"I want to talk to them."

"What happened?" he asks again so I slap his glasses off his face and push him up against the nearest wall. He's startled by my sudden ferocity. "Lavender, I will tell you every detail about my time in Spain, but right now you're gonna pull up your phone and you're gonna get Risina on the line or you are useless to me."

Lavender fishes out his phone, does whatever he has to do dialing-wise, and hands the device to me.

"Hello." Her voice is as anxious as mine.

"Are you safe?"

"Yes. Are you?"

"Yes. I'll be with you soon."

"Okay," she says. I love her more in that moment than I ever have. She knows there are people everywhere listening in on this conversation and there is no way she is going to give any of those bastards the satisfaction of hearing us intimately. That *okay* is worth a billion *I love you*'s.

I lower the phone and hand it back to Lavender. During the exchange with Risina, my eyes scan the street, the parked cars, the windows, the rooftops for any sign of Castillo.

"Where's your car?"

"There." Lavender points to a black Mercedes.

"Give me the keys."

"Why?"

"He's already followed me from one ambush and I'm not going to let him again."

"So Castillo's alive?" he asks, flat, but there's an ounce of recrimination in his voice.

I'm going to give him a pass on that one, but I'll be damned if he's going to get an answer. I hold out my hand and he gives me the keys.

"Find your own way home," I say.

I assume Castillo is already in America. Hunting.

CHAPTER

8

THE ONE SENSE WORTH A DAMN IS TOUCH. YOU CAN LOVE someone without seeing her, without hearing her voice, without smelling her, tasting her, but you'll never know someone, truly know her, until your fingers are intertwined, until your lips explore, until your bodies join, until you touch, then touch, touch, touch, and touch.

I lie in bed and listen to the tub fill in the hotel bathroom. A melody, sung in Italian, wafts slowly from behind the closed door. If Risina is upset by this circumstance, she is hiding it from me.

I get up, lazy and spent, and head into the adjoining suite. Pooley stretches across the width of the bed, a clump of covers and pillows not quite arranged the way intended. He's underneath, breathing and snoring, a stutter-hum that is as beautiful as a ballad. I place my hand on his back, where his pajama top has ridden up almost to his neck, and touch the skin, which is surprisingly hot. He shifts in his sleep but doesn't open his eyes, and I hope whatever is in his dream includes me. Maybe that's selfish, but thoughts unspoken always are.

The faucet in the bathroom quiets, and the melody stops as Risina lowers into the tub, and I can hear her *ahhhhhhhh*, the warm water doing its work on tense muscles. I step inside the door, moments later, and her eyes are closed, the water line up to her chin. She looks gorgeous. Stunning. She always has.

I hop onto the sink counter and watch her bathe.

—⁂—

An hour later, she's heard every detail. Aiza and the wooden toyshop and Ochoa and Angelina and Belmonte and, finally, Castillo and that red file and what it could mean for us. She turns on the faucet with a little more hot water every quarter hour or so, just long enough to reheat the tub. She asks a few questions and I wish I had better answers.

"How long will we stay here?"

"Here" is somewhere in rural Ohio.

"We'll keep you on the move until I find Castillo and kill him."

"Pooley is so young it doesn't matter. But soon . . . he'll be in school. And then we have to ask ourselves, can we continue to do this?"

"I know."

"I don't think we can."

"One day at a time."

She sits up so her breasts are just below the water line. "We have to talk about this when it's over. We can't pretend it's okay anymore. No matter how much this life means to us."

"We'll do it."

"For Pooley."

"Yes."

"You promise?"

"I promise."

"I feel like I failed you. The file . . ."

"The file served its purpose. I'm the one who failed."

"Look at us. A couple of failures." But there's some mirth to her voice. She's always able to laugh at the absurdity. She stands and water cascades off her body back into the tub, onto the floor. "Is the door locked?"

"No."

"Lock it," she says.

She doesn't have to tell me a second time.

⊷⊶

Outside, there's a chill in the air that matches the look on Cargill's face. He's even rounder than when I last saw him in New York when he gave me the Castillo file. He's wearing one of those puffy coats that inspire comparisons to the Michelin man. His nose is red, but his hands stay in his pockets. He makes a point not to wipe. A brown field stretches to the horizon behind the hotel. A cluster of cows dots the landscape, huddled together to fend off the wind. Whatever guests are staying here besides us chose to stay near the fireplaces in their rooms. We have the porch to ourselves.

Cargill cups his hands to light a cigarette, takes a drag, then holds it tucked into his sleeve, a trick veteran smokers master in the Northeast.

"Well, we're in a new position here," he says to jumpstart the conversation.

I keep my expression neutral. "I'll get him."

He raises his eyebrows but doesn't respond. If he wants contrition, he's going to be as disappointed as Lavender was in Spain.

"Do you understand basic accounting?"

I look at him.

"There's not much to it, actually. Numbers are either red, which means we're taking losses, or they're in the black, which means we're doing all right. The account we have with you has always been break-even. What attracted us to the possibility of you was the anonymity of what you provide. No one asks about you. Outside of my tiny division, no eyebrows are raised. Missions are assigned and missions are completed. But now, now we're running in the red and men in high places are asking the questions I sought to avoid."

I turn so our eyes are level. "I'll get him," I repeat, ice in my voice. He steps back, *flinches* might be a better word, then nods.

"So we understand each other?" he adds, because men like him have to have the final word. I let him.

A pair of carrion birds flies lazily over the field, catch sight of something, and start their slow cycle.

Cargill's phone rings and he moves off a few feet to answer with a curt "hello." I watch the sky, the cows, the birds.

Cargill's face turns white, then red again with the bright contrast of a barber's pole. He asks where and how and when and says "I'll be right there. Two hours."

He looks like he's been slapped.

Out in the field, the buzzards drop, land, and awkwardly hobble toward their supper.

The plane is a four-seater, not my favorite mode of travel by any stretch. I've never been a good flyer, and on the big commercial flights I watch with envy as we glide through frame-shaking turbulence and the flight attendants or businessmen go about talking and laughing and watching their movies while my knuckles turn white. I like being in control, I like being armed, and an airplane is the only place where I can't be either. These little planes? Forget it.

I do my best to concentrate on the pilot's seat in front of me, just one section of leather, a scratch carved on its surface, and put all my concentration on that blemish until the wheels touch the ground. It is only Cargill and the pilot and me, so I have the back row to myself and Cargill doesn't feel much like talking. Concentrate, concentrate, just this tiny patch of molested leather and my thoughts and misgivings. *Pop, pop.*

Risina and Pooley remain at the hotel in Ohio, but will move in the morning. No place for more than two nights and we have a series of drop phones we'll use to communicate. We don't trust the government to keep us safe. We never have. We'll make our own arrangements as soon as we can.

The plane touches down at Baltimore–Washington International, a much better alternative to Dulles, and an SUV waits for us. Cargill asks the driver to hand him the keys and find his own way home. I climb into the passenger seat and we don't say a word for the fifty-mile ride on I-95. The silence is pronounced. I don't know what he's thinking, about his job, his partner, my mission, how much his own ledger is in the red now, but he looks shattered. This isn't about departments and dollars and control and power. The world he's kept on the other side of telephones and computer screens and public lunches has reached out and walloped him. His driving is more turbulent than the plane flight, but I'm happy to be on the ground so I don't comment.

We reach an exit for a suburban Virginia subdivision with an innocuous name, Prescott Valley, make a few turns, and draw up to a small stone-and-brick home built by the same architect who designed all the others. A few black SUVs are parked in front, but no police cruisers light up the neighborhood and alert the fine residents of Prescott Valley that there's bloodshed on the block.

We head up the walk and the front door opens and one of the dark men looks at Cargill and steps out of the way.

"Where is he?" he asks a covey of five more men who mill about at the base of a stairwell. One just points up and lowers his eyes.

We trudge up the stairs. Eight more men in suits up here. *How did they get here? What are their jobs? Do they all know who I am?* I mean, I know when I agreed or was blackmailed to work for these people, I'd have a support team with money and power, and yet, I've never been exposed to the number of people amassed in this house. American tax dollars, collected and then *poof,* made to vanish like a magician's white dove, only to reappear again in the form of a bloody mess on the other side of the world. Would you rather not know? Is it better to not know? To stay comfortably numb? I can't answer that for you.

We arrive inside a large bedroom, and I know this is not a bachelor's house. Too big. This is a family's house, so what we see is horrific. Two boys, both young, single-digit ages, dead on the floor, left where they were shot. Their mother sprawls at the foot of the bed, like she was leaping to protect her children but struck down in the act. Against the far wall, propped in the corner, is Lavender, Cargill's partner, the one who picked me up from the jail in Barcelona. He's seated with his legs stretched in front of him, his hands bound behind his back, an entry wound and an exit wound on either side of his head.

Stupid Lavender. Poor, stupid Lavender. Castillo followed us out of the jail after all but I naïvely thought he would focus on me. I left Lavender on the sidewalk, told him to find his own way home, thank-you-very-much, and executed an exit plan that would shake even the most stubborn tail. But dammit, Castillo didn't need to follow me, not when he could bird-dog Lavender all the way back to the United States, all the way to this house in the suburbs of D.C. And what information did he hope to gain? Why did he force Lavender to watch his family executed? Did he want to know who hired me, who put his name on the top of the page? Why he was my target? How Lavender was involved?

And did he get answers to any of these questions?

If he simply wanted Lavender to give me up, to make a deal, my life for his family, then Lavender miscalculated how far Castillo would go. Every killing tells a story, but this one has a lot of open-ended questions.

Cargill collects his emotions and then a flinty hardness settles over him, like putting on a suit of armor. "Anything taken from this room that is not in this room now?" he barks at no one in particular.

A damn good question, I think. Maybe I've underestimated Cargill.

One of the dark men coughs into his fist and speaks up, diffident. "There was a sheet of paper on the carpet. Like maybe it was left by the killer. We're running it through analysis downstairs as we—"

"I told you not to touch ANYTHING!" Cargill snaps. The house goes immediately silent.

"The director requested it but if you want to call him—" the man says, a pass-the-buck threat.

Cargill's cheeks are the color of brick, filled with blood. He'd make a terrible gambler, the way his face flushes. He lowers his voice and growls "Show it to me." He takes one last look at the macabre tableau and heads out after the man. I'm not sure he's aware I am here.

In the kitchen, some kind of mobile tech unit has set up monitors running encryption software and tapped into some kind of sophisticated system designed to keep secrets in and hackers out. A single sheet of paper lies on a light board. Several dark men step out of the way to let Cargill move close. His face scrunches up as he reads what is there, a stumped student staring at a chalkboard.

"This mean anything to you?" he tosses over his shoulder and it takes a moment for me to realize he's addressing me. I feel every eye in the room shift my way, and I do not like the feeling. I'm fond of shadows, not spotlights.

The page is information, meaningless to everyone but me. And it hits me: this entire scene, the tragedy upstairs, four lives snuffed out including a woman and two boys who were not involved, was for me. It was not about learning something from Lavender. His fate was sealed no matter what came out of his mouth. Castillo murdered this family so I would come here, see what he knows.

The page is from the red file, the one he showed me on the Calle Cadiz after he stuffed his fence's head into the trunk of my rental car. Where Aiza got his information, how he got it, from whom he bought it, I don't know, but this page, this fucking page, shows that my life is not as secret as I thought.

The page provides information regarding Jacqueline Owens, now Jacqueline Hamilton, whom I knew as Jake. She lives in Colorado with her husband and seven-year-old boy. It supplies her address, her place of employment, her phone number, a photo.

At the bottom, in Spanish, it reads "Was intimate with Columbus before recruitment." Then in red ink, circled: "I wonder if he loves her."

I take the paper, snatch it right off the light board, and when others try to stop me, Cargill waves them down. I don't know how he stands on his accounting ledger, but I know he's right there next to me, bathed in red ink. The only chance he has to avenge his partner is to unchain me. It's personal for both of us now.

I drive for fifteen straight hours. No more flights, no need to rush, time to get my mind right. I cross the state line into Arkansas and a trooper pulls behind me, his lights flashing, and then after a moment he turns them off and falls away. He must have radioed in my license plate and whatever message came over his computer screen said a version of "leave this driver alone."

The drop phone I have doesn't handle Bluetooth, so I press it to my ear, one hand on the wheel.

I fill her in and her voice is heavy. "How do you know he hasn't hurt her?"

"He's using Jake as bait. Wiggle the worm and wait for me to bite. I know because I've done it before." I had, with her.

"He's a terrible man. I know it. I sensed it when I was in Spain, putting the file together for you. And maybe that is why I did not do my best work. Perhaps my instinct kicked in, the kind, you know, that says there is danger lurking nearby, the kind that makes you get out your keys and put them between your knuckles in an underground garage, you know? I stopped poking in holes and maybe my cowardice is why you're in this position."

"Risina, your file got me to the target the way it always does. I made a mess and now I have to clean it up. You did nothing wrong. The mess was my making. Not yours."

I hear my wife blow an exasperated breath I can feel through the phone. In my mind, she pushes her hair out of her eyes.

"I miss you," she says.

"I miss you too, Risina. You think you know, but you don't know."

"I love you. Pooley loves you. Kill this man so you can come home to us." And that is why I adore this woman so much. I love you and kill this man in the same breath.

———

Jacqueline Owens, Jake, is the first woman I loved. She was in my life in Boston before my name was Columbus and my first fence counseled me to break things off with her but I didn't listen. I thought I could keep my personal life a secret, but secrets in this game are like divers' bubbles. They take a long time to reach the surface, but eventually they arrive there and pop. They always do.

Innocently, Jake stumbled upon me while I was ingratiating myself with two thugs in order to kill their boss, and her life was threatened. To ensure her safety, I convinced her I was terrible for her and persuaded her to leave Boston. We have not spoken since, though I did track her down once to see if she was okay. She was. She was married. She was happy. That was many years ago, before Risina, before my son.

And now she has been thrust back into the game as if what I did back then didn't matter. As if all these years I sacrificed did not matter. An innocent woman, far removed from my killing life, now bait to lure me into the open.

I drive because I need the time to rage. I know it will come, the anger, the white-hot passionate fury that is my enemy, the enemy of clarity, and I have to get it out now so I can leave it behind and sharpen my focus. But not now. Now is searing wrath. Now is scarlet vehemence. I'm going to kill Castillo. This man who thinks he knows me and wants to shove in my face the pages of my history. I'm going to hurt him. I'm going to make his death painful. Punishment is coming.

Do you still want the lie? We're nearing the end and you're welcome to leave me here, driving west again, everyone I love now, everyone I loved then, still alive. You can stop reading and go on with your life and it'll stay that way forever. Yes, not knowing may eat at you but not knowing can also protect your sanity, keep your faith that all stories have a natural progression toward light. The popular ones do, at least.

But you know it's not true. Tragedy is life's arc. It has always been so. The ones who fall gently into death, surrounded by friends and family? They're a mirage, a bubble, the tale the preacher tells to get you to go along with the rest of the sheep. Few find happiness. The great, great majority run headlong and blindly into sorrow. The bubble pops. The reaper waits for all of us, and everyone we've adored.

The truth is coming. I can't give you what you ask anymore. Not after seeing that page from my file, the accuracy of the information, the specificity, the knowledge there are more pages like it in Castillo's possession. I'm too angry to protect you, to make up lies so you can sleep tonight. The truth is a monster and it feels no remorse.

I check into a hotel in Greeley, Colorado, half an hour from Boulder, where Jake lives. It's one of those blocky, cheap, homogenous structures that have sprung up in every big-city suburb in the South and Midwest. It might be a Fairview or a Days Inn or a Comfort Inn or an Embassy Suites. I'm not here for comfort. I'm here to shower and sleep and prepare myself for tomorrow.

I know he's already watching Jake, waiting for me, a hunter in his forest blind, the field seeded. Or rather, he's watching everything around her, waiting for me to make a move. I hope I haven't overestimated his patience.

The next morning, I drive to a sporting-goods store and buy a plain black pair of sweat pants and a logoless windbreaker, a new pair of sunglasses, and a gray golf hat. Nothing to stand out, nothing memorable. I then head to the Denver International Airport and leave Cargill's government SUV in the parking lot and rent an egg-white, no-frills sedan, the vehicle equivalent of an invisibility cloak. Risina booked it for me, so I don't have to talk to anyone but the ancient man at the guard booth. He beckons me forward like Charon, takes a quick look at the paperwork, the gate opens, and I head out toward Boulder.

She lives in a neighborhood near Chautauqua Park, in a contemporary home on an ample lot. There is no white picket fence but there might as well be. The years must've been good to her. She's settled in.

I drive to 12th Street, keep my head forward and relaxed while my eyes search for any anomalies, cars parked where they're not supposed to be, movement in trees, strange joggers or pedestrians. Castillo probably changed his appearance, so I can't dismiss anyone. I keep my speed locked and the wheel steady. I only drive the street once. If he's in a stakeout position, I don't want him to make note of the same sedan looping through here, as inconspicuous as it may be.

There's an Audi Q5 in Jake's driveway, a silver SUV, this year's model. The house is quiet. I drive on, find a grocery store a few streets away, and camp out inside, wandering the aisles while I think this through. A woman pushing a cart with a shaky wheel turns down my aisle, too old to be Jake but I wonder how many times she has come here over the years, to this store, this aisle, so close to her house.

I think of a number of scenarios to approach her front door, but can I risk his response or her reaction when I knock? The alarm in the back of my mind tells me I've been in this store too long. I buy a box of protein bars and milk and a few Cokes for the caffeine and move to the register to pay. A fire truck pulls into the lot outside and several firefighters disembark and head inside, laughing about some collective joke only they understand. I look at their truck, an idea forming.

A pair of vehicles roars up to Jake's house, lights flashing, a fire engine and a truck. A dozen firefighters climb off, walk with purpose, and snatch equipment out of panels on the side of the apparatus. It's a swarm of activity, men dressed in bulky uniforms and helmets, impossible to distinguish individually.

The front door opens and a woman and her boy emerge. I'd recognize her anywhere. The hairstyle has changed, the clothes are different, but her eyes, her lips, even the expression of surprise and bewilderment on her face are the same as those worn by the girl I knew in Boston all those years ago. I tear my eyes from her to watch the perimeter. My gaze drifts to the trees, the neighboring windows, the street. Residents come out of their houses, drawn to the blinking red lights the way they always are, the world over.

He's watching. I can feel it.

The situation is chaotic, and he knows it is manufactured. He feels me and I feel him.

The firefighters huddle around Jake and she holds her son's hand, pulls him in tight by her hip, protective. More neighbors gather in the street and I join them and search the faces but I don't see him. I'm only forty feet from Jake and I don't want to look at her, afraid of what will happen if she recognizes me. The firefighters persuade Jake to let them inside to check things out and a couple of them open her front door and disappear through it. I can hear Jake ask what happened and a fireman tells her someone called 911 about smoke in her attic.

A black car with tinted windows barrels around the corner and heads for the house. It cuts through traffic and screeches this way with purpose, a guided missile, dodging lookie-loos who have gathered in the street, hoping for free entertainment. They're about to get it.

The car blitzes up, honking, which doesn't fit the bill for Castillo, but he might be making some kind of countermove. The car nearly clips me as it ducks into the driveway and slams on its brakes next to the fire truck. The driver pops out, a large man, worried. The husband. Jake's husband.

He hurries out of his car and bolts over to Jake, who is happy to see him, relieved to see him. He can be in charge of dealing with this shit rather than she, and she's happy to pass it off to him and head back inside with her boy. I look at them, this family, this suburban trio with a nice house in a middle-class neighborhood, this Norman Rockwell picture of contentment and I think: *this could have been me. If Hap Blowenfeld had never walked into my life, this could have been me.* And it hits me, right in the middle of this absurd moment, I am pleased. I ran from this normality. I see it now. This. This isn't me. This has never been me.

Jake has her hands out in that gesture of *I have no idea how this happened* and her husband tries to shush her as he engages with the fire chief and the chief shrugs and seems to agree this is all just a false-alarm misunderstanding and these words are on his lips when Jake's husband's head explodes.

Even as experienced as I am, this shot catches me flat-footed. I did not consider that Castillo would meet chaos with chaos. He guesses I'm here so he opens fire on the husband, assuming I'll make a move to protect Jake, and he's right, I bolt for her with the knowledge that shots are about to follow, though I still haven't spotted Castillo in the crowd.

Gawkers scream to the right of me and spread away from the shooter like ripples from a stone tossed into still water, and the fire chief, brave fool that he is, rushes *toward* the assassin, while a second firefighter stoops to assist the dead husband who will never need assistance again. I sprint for Jake and in one hand I scoop up her boy and with the other, I shoulder her toward her front door, and a shot comes and whistles past my ear but it's too late, we're through the door and I mule-kick it closed behind us as the three of us crash to the marble floor of the foyer.

As soon as Jake is free of me, she scrambles for her son and pulls him into her chest and her eyes go to my face like a wolf ready to tear into a predator threatening her cub, and there is a moment I can read her mind as it catches up to what her eyes tell her.

"No," she says. "No. Nononononono . . ." Each word comes out more severe than the last, an orchestra percussion building to a crescendo.

"Jake." It's all I can think of to say.

"No! No! No!" She's furious, her eyes flashing hot and her son starts screaming. Hysterical.

The front door starts to open and I smash it closed with my foot and yell over the kid's wailing, "We have to move!"

Two firefighters choose that moment to descend the stairs, the two who came inside to search the attic for smoking embers, oblivious to what had happened in the driveway. I completely forgot about them and here they are, taking in the scene at the base of the stairs: a woman and child on the floor, huddled together, screaming, and a wild man stretched out, holding the door closed with his foot.

Their radios sound at the same time with a *shots fired! shots fired!* and I can see both of them launch into protection mode as their training kicks in.

"Wait! Wait!" I say, but neither obeys. They descend the stairs, heavy boots churning, and a bullet splinters the door above my head but they don't notice, so focused are they on me. The closest one says something like *hey, pal* and his hands reach my shirt and he's much stronger than I would have suspected. He lifts me as easily as if he is hoisting a hose and pins my back to the front door, next to the fresh bullet hole. He has no idea what's on the other side of the door, and he holds me there with his meaty forearm, stapling my neck to the wood. He turns to Jake with some version of *is this guy bothering you, ma'am?* or *do you know this man?* and she grapples to answer but a second bullet rips through the door, this one fired from close range, and it zips by my other ear and lifts the firefighter off his feet, catching him in the side of the head and clearing through his opposite eye. As he sprawls sideways, his partner looks at me like I just performed some kind of magic trick. I see that click in his eyes when shock turns to rage.

Jake pulls her child into her chest and covers his eyes, an instinct every living creature shares, protect the young. She scoots backward, still on the floor, still sitting, just propelling herself in reverse while she clutches the child, *get away, get away, get away* her only thoughts I'm sure, but I can't concentrate on her because I have Castillo on one side of a flimsy door and a confused and pissed-off fireman raising his halligan bar above his head like a caveman's club. In a close-contact fight with more than one opponent, neutralize the most immediate threat first. Live to fight another day as the saying goes, and most sayings become sayings because they hit upon a universal truth. As the fireman lifts his halligan to the apex of its arc, I pull my Glock from the small of my back and swing it, a right hook with two pounds of high-strength nylon-based polymer as a makeshift set of brass knuckles and I connect just under his chin. His helmet flies and the halligan drops to the marble floor and he stumbles back against the stairs, and sorry, friend, I admire you and your job, but you're in my way so I pop him three more times, taking some teeth with the last blow, because this son-of-a-bitch is tough and even beaten, he tries to stand up but his legs won't let him.

I lose sight of Jake in the thirty seconds it takes to dispatch the fireman and suddenly an ear-splitting alarm rises up from the uniform of his partner, the one shot in the head at close range, an alarm that signals when a man is down, incapacitated, a signal for his buddies to come rescue him. It's a hell of a sound, a sharp, piercing chirp that threatens to wipe out all thought. It is so loud I almost don't hear the window crash open in the adjoining room; in fact, I'm not sure I hear it so much as catch the movement in my periphery.

Castillo is in the house.

It's only a matter of minutes before half the first responders in Boulder are in here too.

I bolt forward, further inside the home, the direction Jake and her son must've gone, hoping I get to them first. I don't know the layout of the house. I know it is mid-sized but it seems sprawling on the inside, and there must be a million nooks and crannies here but when I get to the kitchen, she's standing in the corner, her son tucked behind her, holding a butcher's knife, shivering, terrified. Her eyes are as wild as a tiger's.

I open my mouth to say her name but the firefighter alarm is deafeningly loud, even in the kitchen here and so whatever I try to say is lost. I step closer and she raises the knife. Then a warning flashes in her wild eyes and instinctively I pivot just as Castillo enters the kitchen. I catch his gun hand with my shoulder and the pistol fires. The bullet ricochets off the refrigerator and plugs into the wall, and for the second time we look at each other face to face, our noses inches apart. He is the hunter and I am the hunter and one of us is going to die at the other's hand. It is as clear as if it were written in a holy book. He's my height and my weight and if his skin were darker, we could be father and son. His eyes are black, inked with darkness, and his breath is hot and smells like cigars. I hate him. I hate him more than I've ever hated a mark and he will pay in blood for soiling my past.

The firefighter's alarm suddenly stops which means more firefighters are in the house, moving his body to quiet the alarm, and as I wrestle for leverage with Castillo, I spy Jake out of the corner of my eye snatch up a set of keys not five feet from where I am fighting this killer, and she ducks out a door next to the kitchen table.

I grit my teeth and turn my full attention to Castillo, my hands holding his wrists as they thrash and flail, and I'm aware I'm growling like a dog. He's stronger than me, but I've been scrapping a long time. He tries to push me into the island and I employ one of the oldest dirty tricks: I drop my resistance so his weight rushes forward and then use his momentum against him, flip him around so it is his back against the island. This is the precise moment when a firefighter's axe whips down into my line of sight. It only misses Castillo's head by a whisker, and I'm so surprised I reverse off him as two more firefighters and a cop swarm Castillo like zombies ganging up on a stumbling man. I don't wait to see more. My feet propel me through the door Jake slipped through ten seconds ago.

The garage door is up and she has strapped her son into the toddler's seat in the back of her minivan. Even in her panic, she is thinking of her child's safety. That's the Jake I remember.

She screams as I rip the keys right out of her hand, but before she can rake me with her fingernails, I slide behind the wheel and scream "get in!" She is torn but I have her child in here with me and there really is no decision.

"Now!" I bellow louder, and she snaps out of her stupor, hurries around the van into the passenger seat while she repeats *please, please, please*. As soon as the door closes, I mash the accelerator and explode out of the garage in reverse.

The boy, AJ, short for Alex Jr., stops crying and falls asleep.

Jake, too, appears cried out. Her head is turned to the window, though I don't think she's sleeping. Outside, the wheat fields of Kansas roll by with only a few fences to distinguish one from another. The moon is out, full and judgmental, and the road is lit. I detour off the Interstate and take a farm-to-market road. An hour goes by before I see a brake light or headlight.

Jake's head turns and I feel her eyes study me. I feel the pull but do not look over. I can't.

She says my name. My real name. The one before Columbus, before I walked into the Columbus Textile Company warehouse and came out a killer. She says it again, sharper.

"Yes?"

"Why?"

"Why what?"

"Why'd you bring this back to me? Why now?"

"Jake . . ."

"It's Jacqueline," she says bitterly. "Jake died in an apartment in Boston, broken on the floor. Gut-punched. Kicked."

I can't fault her for that. I know the importance of shedding a name, even if it's for your own sanity. Jake, Jacqueline, is referring to the last time we spoke, when we were both younger and I realized she couldn't be a part of my life. I told you this story before, when I first started telling you about me, when I still did my best to tell you the truth.

"Jacqueline," I try again, "I didn't mean for this to happen. The entire reason I did what I did back in Boston was to prevent this from happening."

"Oh, okay," she snorts, rolling her eyes.

"If you want to hear the truth, I'll give you the truth. You deserve it. If you don't, fine, I'll shut up or tell you whatever you want to hear. I'm fine either way."

"My husband is dead!" she hisses, trying to keep her voice down so AJ will sleep but the emotion overwhelms her and she cries again with angry, growling heaves.

"I know and I'm not happy about that."

"You're not happy? *You're* not happy!"

"I didn't mean—"

"Fuck you!" she hurls and turns back to the window, and AJ wakes up and says *mommy, mommy, mommy* over and over in a rhythm with her sobbing and she doesn't have the strength to soothe him.

We find a motel in Salina, Kansas, and I pull her car into the parking lot and stop in a blank row away from congestion. The sun will be up soon and the sky has a pink-and-blue tint that promises comfort but rarely delivers.

I cut the engine and the car falls silent. She hasn't said a word for the last couple of hours and when the car stops, she raises herself like she's hoisting her body from a dark pit. She blinks a few times, and I'm not sure she knows where she is. Comprehension soon returns, and with it, sorrow.

"Go," I say.

She looks out the back windshield at the motel's reception office and, next to it, a 24-hour diner with only a few booths occupied. She opens her door, hesitates. "You're not going to take off as soon as I get out?"

I shake my head.

"If you do—"

"I won't."

She steels herself, unsure, then rushes around behind the car and opens AJ's door. "Come on, baby," she says as she unbuckles him from the car seat. He stirs, sleepy, and shifts his weight to her. They've done this enough times to do it in their sleep, and soon she has him in her arms, and she shuts the door with her hip.

I watch in the rearview mirror as she quick-steps across the parking lot, cradling her child in that reverse-piggyback all parents know. I plan to watch her all the way into the diner, but she stops before she walks ten paces from the car.

For what seems an eternity, she stands in place, like she's seen Medusa's face, the neon of the FREE WIFI sign bathing her in a soft, hazy light. AJ opens his eyes and they find mine in the mirror and I can clearly see his mother in him, or at least his mother from before I kicked her in the stomach. Before she knew to fear men.

Jake turns and crosses back to me, approaches the driver's side window, and raps it with her knuckles. I have to turn the engine on to lower it.

"You know I'm going to walk in there, ask for a phone, and dial 911."

"I thought you might."

"Then why'd you let me go? Why aren't you speeding away?"

"I'm tired."

"You want to be caught?"

"It doesn't matter if you call."

"Why?"

I don't answer.

"Why? You owe me that."

"Jake." And she doesn't correct me this time. "It doesn't matter if you call because I work for them. And they want the man who shot your husband. Not me."

"Who shot Alex?"

"The man I was fighting in your kitchen. It's a long story . . ."

"Do you think I'm going to sleep if I don't know it?" she roars and AJ starts crying again. "Hush," she says, only less vehemently by a degree. "Will I ever hear it if you drive away? Because I spent the last fifteen years not knowing why you did what you did to me. And it has eaten at me every day, every hour since I saw you last. And today, today you show up as suddenly, as jarringly, as you fucking left, like the nightmare I've had a thousand times, and my husband is *dead*, my happiness is *over*, and if I walk across that parking lot, if I go in there and call 911, well, goddammit, this is my last chance, my *only* chance to know. And I can't live with that. How can I go on living with that? I won't do it again. I won't. Hush. Honey, hush now. I won't."

She runs out of steam, and her shoulders sag. I see the need, the desperation.

We check into a motel room, and I tell the truth until my throat hurts.

CHAPTER

9

MY PHONE IS OFF AND I SHOULD CALL AND CHECK IN WITH Cargill and check in with Risina but the road is non-judgmental and infinite and placid. It is nothing and I feel nothing and the country is nothing and my debt is everything. I've taken, I've taken, I've taken and now I owe. I took when I was young and didn't know better, and

I took when I was older and knew it was dangerous, and I'm taking now because to stop would make a mockery of fortune. Truth is a monster and its teeth are sharp and it demands blood. My blood, your blood, Christ's blood, and there is no absolution, no Sunday, no third day, no resurrection, no forgiveness, not for me. The rearview mirror is four inches from my face but I haven't looked into it since I left the motel, I won't look into it, because the eyes staring back at me won't be my own and I might start screaming and never stop.

Up ahead, the two-lane highway arrives at an unexpected stop sign, with a single red bulb suspended above it by timeworn wires and two wooden poles wedged into place before I was born. I slow before I reach it, perfunctorily, involuntarily, some vestige of obedience embedded inside me from before.

I stop.

There are no other cars on the highway, just an intersection with spokes that stretch to everywhere and nowhere. The light blinks on, off, on, off, on. Pop, pop, pop, pop, pop.

I cut the engine. I open the driver's door and emerge from the car like a cavalry soldier dismounting his horse. My feet touch the ground.

The red light blinks on, off, on.

I raise my Glock and aim.

On, off, on, off, on, off . . . and in that half-second as it blinks on again, I fire, and the shot is the only sound in the world, and the light shatters, pieces of plastic shower to the pavement like water from a faucet and I drop to my knees so hard and unexpectedly that my bones start to throb.

It'll be over soon. It'll be over soon. It'll be over soon, says the pain. On, off, on.

I look at the stop sign on the side of the road and notice two bullet holes in the "s" and the "p."

Someone with a gun was here before me.

When I turn my phone on, there's a text with a number. I press it and thumb DIAL NUMBER and wait for the line to connect.

"Where are you?" Cargill's voice.

"I don't know," I answer and that might be the truest thing I've said in a long time.

"I need to see you. Immediately." There's an edge to his voice that sounds manufactured, false. Like he has to play a character out of his range now.

"Where?"

"D.C. The Plaza Hotel. Room 2223. Knock two times and I'll answer."

I hang up, put the phone under the rear tire, and roll over it as I guide the car back onto the blacktop.

Risina and Pooley are in Tennessee, in a safe house east of Memphis. The dark men have been inept about a number of things but they are well versed in moving and hiding. I guess they've spent a lot of energy plotting their own escapes.

I unbox a second drop phone, connect it to the cigarette lighter, and dial the series of numbers Risina and I pre-planned.

"How is he?" I ask.

"Remarkably well adjusted," she answers. "How are you?"

"Remarkably not."

"You saw Castillo? Face to face?"

"Yes."

"Describe him to me."

"He looked like me."

She absorbs that. Then, "I'm scared. I'm really scared." I know she wants me to say I am too, but I can't.

"Risina—"

"Don't say it."

"Risina—"

"Don't, please."

"I have to."

"Oh, god. Oh, god. Not yet. I'm not ready."

I hear rustling through the phone, though I don't know what makes the sound. I wait until I hear her breath on the line again. Her voice sounds different.

"I am grateful for the time we had together," she says, and I don't stop her or comfort her or say, *shhhhhhh, everything's going to be all right.* I've been in this business too long to believe it. "I am so, so grateful to you for Pooley and for pulling my nose out of books and giving me these last few years." Her voice is thick. "I know you only have one opportunity for this life, I know that, and maybe I'll suffer in the next for what I've done but I will not suffer here. I will not."

We fooled ourselves. We laughed and we pretended and we lied to each other, willingly. And it could've gone on like that forever.

Before Pooley.

Once our son arrived, her love split as it should have. As is natural.

"I love you."

"I know."

"When?"

"As soon as I get the chance."

"This is it, then."

"This is it. Tonight, tomorrow. The next day. When no one is looking."

"We won't talk again."

"No. I can't put him on the phone. I won't let this be his last interaction with you."

"No."

For a minute or maybe twenty or maybe a lifetime or just a few breaths we say nothing and there is nothing and the world is nothing and Risina and I are nothing.

For our son.

For the first time, I know how Jake felt, kicked in the stomach, cracked in the nose, all those years ago.

"Listen to me. Tell Pooley, when he's older, when he's much older, twenty years from now, tell him to go to the barbershop in the basement of the St. Regis Hotel in New York . . ."

"Baby—"

"No, listen. This is important. Tell him to go to that barbershop and ask for the owner. Tell him to tell whoever it is at the time to give him a package addressed to Pooley from my real name."

"What're you talking about?"

"Can you do that, Risina?"

"I—"

"Can you do that?" I shout, louder than I mean to.

"What is the package?" she asks calmly, like a therapist trying to talk a patient off a ledge.

"An account of my life. Everything. The good and the bad. Everything."

"I'm going to go now." I can hear the terrible despondency in her voice. "I'm going to go and this will be it."

"I understand."

"I will love you forever. But I have to tell Pooley the lie. I have to make up who you were, even when he's older."

"You don't have to. It is there if you want it."

"I love you."

"I love you so much."

Then neither of us wants to say it, so we listen to the other's breathing.

At some point, the line goes dead, but I'm not sure if I pressed END or she did.

———

The Potomac is the gray-green color of decaying flesh. I park Jake's car in one of the ubiquitous public parking spots along the river and walk a half block in the sticky, stifling air to a bus stop. What is it about humans that when we're suffering on the inside, we seek discomfort in the world? I could've driven directly to the Plaza, or parked next to a taxi stand or just left the car in the middle of K Street and stolen another, but here I sit, at a bus stop, surrounded by a cloud of mosquitos, a trash can to my left overflowing with detritus.

After twenty minutes, a city bus swooshes to a stop and the driver looks at me, bored, wary. "Well?" he asks, one hand on the lever that closes the doors.

The question registers somewhere in the soup of my thoughts and I stand and climb aboard. The bus is half-full, a piece of the ebb between the morning commute and lunch. I choose a seat in the back and the driver eyes me a few extra seconds before he wedges back into traffic. A woman a few seats ahead plays with her phone, another has earbuds in her ears and bobs her head. Together and apart. There's a Steinbeck book about riders on a bus but I can't remember the title. Another stop and a dwarf embarks and makes his way down the aisle, smiling the whole way. When he reaches me, he stops and asks, "Do I know you?"

I shake my head and he points a finger gun at me and says, "My bad, brother" and keeps on going to the back row. I turn to look at him again and he smiles at me with teeth that seem too large for his face.

The Washington Plaza Hotel is on Thomas Circle, a stone's throw from the White House. It looks and feels like the rest of D.C.: functional, outdated, monolithic. I stop in the gift shop and buy pants, a plain shirt, not too garish, socks, underwear, and a hat.

"Lost your luggage?" the clerk asks. "Happens alllll the time."

I smile and nod. I hope Cargill doesn't mind me taking a shower, because I am ready to wash this week, this mission, this assignment, this life off of me.

The hallway on the twenty-second floor is empty. I follow the sign around a corner and down a long stretch where the numbers count up in twos, 2211, 2213, 2215 until I get to the right one. The door is propped open by the security latch, flipped between the jamb and the door.

He said to knock. I'm certain of it. And Cargill is as likely to change his tactics as a spider to stop spinning webs. My weapon is out and I already know I have to get out of this hotel with its bubble cams in the hallways and I can smell blood and trouble.

I push the door open with my left hand, my head oscillating, open for surprises, but my ability to react is hampered by these tight quarters. Every voice inside me screams *get the hell out of here, run, regroup, he's already gotten to Lavender, what made you think he couldn't get to Cargill?* Yet here I am, moving inside the room when I should be in the stairwell.

Cargill is tied to the desk chair, his face streaked with blood. A nail juts out of his forehead, and attached to it is another page from Aiza's book. I approach, my feet heavy, like I'm slogging through an ice floe. I can read the page, I'm close enough, but half of it is soaked through with blood. I make out words: Risina. A son. Our address. Her picture.

The page jerks suddenly as Cargill takes in a lungful of air and fresh blood pours out of his nose and mouth. His eyes roll and surface, roll and surface, trying to find a life preserver.

They locate my face and the lids are half-closed and rinsed with blood so the irises bob and droop. He tries to open his mouth but the lips pucker and flatten like a fish on a stringer dumped on the riverbank. The nail is too far inside his skull.

In the bathroom, I find a cup, fill it with water from the sink, and return to him. I put it to his lips and he sucks at it like a newborn trying to latch on to a nipple. His bloody eyes drift to the ceiling, disconnected from the rest of his face.

I have to get out of here. Lick my wounds, take a big step backward, and figure out how to switch from defense to offense. It flipped somewhere in Pasaia and I've been on my heels ever since. No more. If I—

"I hadddddddd . . ." Cargill grunts and when I look over, his scarlet eyes have found me. They follow me across the room as I kneel in front of him and return the cup to his lips. He pushes it aside with his head like a horse nudging his owner's hand.

"I haddddddddd . . ." A struggle to get it out but he has the look of a man with a mile left in a marathon, determined to finish even though his legs are letting him down. His tongue flickers and he wipes away blood on his lips, his teeth. His eyes list again, and then steady as his face shakes, the nail in his temple ticking like a metronome. His voice strengthens and he says "I had to tell him."

Panic rises.

"Tell him what?" I ask.

"Tell him where your family is hiding."

I'm out the door before the last word dies on his lips.

———

She does not pick up her phone, even when I dial the panic code. We are no longer connected, the connection is severed, I made the connection and the connection is gone.

I hope she left me, left her protection detail, escaped with Pooley to a place of her choosing, and she slipped away in time. That was the plan.

I end the call and dial an agency number. The line picks up without ringing and there is no voice this time, just some metallic clicks, so I say "This is Columbus. Cargill's dead. Come pick me up." And then I disconnect the line but leave the phone on.

I walk across the street, sit down on a bus bench in the stifling heat, not far from the hotel.

A black car pulls up less than five minutes later.

They don't know where she is and I take comfort in that. She was supposed to meet her detail in front of the house to transfer to a location on the other side of the state but she did not show up. After ten minutes, the driver and two marshals moved inside to check on Risina and Pooley but both had vanished with no sign of a struggle.

I know she planned to run, but I also know Castillo learned of her location. So which happened first? Will I ever know?

No sign of a struggle gives me hope. Risina would've only gone kicking and screaming, right? Or would she have been submissive if Pooley's life hung in the balance? Not knowing is back, angry, hungry. Not knowing has friends: hopelessness, outrage, insanity.

I sit in an unfurnished office east of the city, about eight stories high judging from the view out the windows. In the room, there is scaffolding, a few paint cans and a drop cloth, but it looks like these are for show, in case any civilians make it up here by mistake. That seems unlikely. The dark men had to buzz in, swipe cards, and submit to fingerprint scanners at least a half-dozen times to arrive on this floor. I was shown a chair and then left alone with not knowing for company.

A woman enters, asks a series of questions about my travel, my aliases, my weapons, the events of today, and then leaves without smiling.

"I could use some water," I say to no one.

A man enters, hands me a plastic bottle with the cap already off, and leaves through the same door as the woman.

How many people watch me right now? I have no idea. I imagine the series of checks and confirmations and digs and clearances and phone calls and computer sweeps going on to determine who the hell I am and how I am tied to Lavender and Cargill. The problem with secret divisions of secret organizations is the secrets die with the men who possess them. I drink the water in one greedy draught.

A moment passes, the door opens, and the same woman enters and sits in front of me. Her hair is down and the top couple of buttons on her blouse are open to show me the tops of her breasts and a hint of the brassiere holding them together. It's insulting but I'm not going to tell her that. I'd rather try to get as much information out of her as I can, and let her think she's doing the same to me.

"How long have you been working for Johnson and Tanners?"

"Who?"

"How long?"

"Well, I knew them as Lavender and Cargill, and they recruited me three years ago."

She checks her tablet, her finger swiping and tapping.

"What were your missions?"

"All of them?"

"Yes."

"Have you found my wife and son?"

She looks up from her iPad. "Your missions?"

"When you answer my question, I'll tell you everything you want to know."

She stands up, agitated, makes a show of closing her tablet cover, and leaves through the same door.

———

Hours later, the door opens and a man with a smooth gait steps in. I can tell who he is by watching his stride, as familiar as a fingerprint.

"Say hey, Columbus," he says.

"Archie," I answer, and even though I don't mean to, I smile.

Archibald Grant was my fence before Risina. He's a true character in a business full of false ones, an original, and he's very good at playing a fool when he's the smartest one in the room. He fell in with the same dark men who recruited me, and was instrumental in pulling me back into this life when I thought I was out. We parted ways immediately after, and I haven't seen him since Pooley was born. Until now.

"You don't look too good."

"Yeah, well, I've been better."

"You got a lotta people here all worked up. People lookin' for shadows to hide in and nothing but spotlights pointing their way everywhere they turn. These folks don't like lights."

"Where's that leave me?"

"Damned if I know. I avoid these folks best I can. They woke me out of a good sleep at five-thirty this morning. Said they had a *situation*. Funny thing, first name to pop in my head was yours."

"I'm flattered."

"For a guy no one knows, you're a guy everyone knows."

"My mark found a file on me."

"Say what?"

"My assignment is to kill an assassin named Castillo. You know him?"

"Not personally, but that name's around on folks' lips."

"I closed in on him in Spain, but he sniffed me out and dodged the bullet. Then he realized I got to him through his fence—"

"Who?"

"Aiza."

Archie makes that *pssss* sound, like it hurt his ears to hear that name. "That fat fuck couldn't fence his way out of a paper bag."

"That fat fuck's head was found in the trunk of my rental sedan. Castillo wasn't happy his fence betrayed him."

Archie nods. "Makes sense."

"But the problem is," I continue, "*my* problem is Aiza kept a file on me, and it is way more explicit and comprehensive than I would've expected."

"How do you know?"

"Because Castillo has it, and he's leaving pages of it behind at his kills like goddamn bread crumbs. He knows about my childhood, he knows about Risina, he knows about my boy."

"I barely know that shit and you *worked* for me. How the hell is two-ton headless Aiza gonna collect all that? Huh?"

"You tell me," I say.

He looks up to see if I'm accusing him but my expression is inscrutable.

"If it's going back to your childhood, I'm gonna guess Vespucci sold his files before he keeled over. How he kept up with you beyond that is a mystery, though I've been surprised before. Lotta people out there make you think they's one way, but behind closed doors they a hell of a lot sharper than they let on."

"Yeah, I know the type."

He leans back in his chair. "These folks want me to bring you in from the cold. Seems like the handlers handling you may have been operating on they own." He checks to see if I'm learning this or have known all along. The truth is I don't care. The dark men gave me assignments, missions, whatever, same as always, and they provided me with support when I needed it, like the jail in Barcelona.

"Okay, I'm in. I'll cooperate. I turned myself in, don't forget. They want me to start filling in blanks? Give me a pen. I'll tell them everything from the day me and you sat down with these people up until the Plaza Hotel yesterday. I just want to know if Risina and Pooley are safe. I already asked them that."

"They told me to tell you they are, they're safe, but I'll tell you the truth: they have no idea. So tell you what, Columbus. I'm gonna go find out what's what. The *real* what's what. It might take me a day. Two on the outside. Can you sit tight until then?"

"I could get out of here and find out myself."

"Hey, man," he says, spreading his arms. "We all gotta compromise."

He gets up and strides back to the door but it opens before he reaches it and the woman with the cleavage steps in front of him. Her body language is brusque and confrontational, arms crossed, legs stiff.

I can't hear the words but she gives Archie an earful.

———

I sleep but it's unsatisfying. I eat but the food has no taste. Worry crowds my senses, so the world filters through a dark net. One day becomes two, and if two becomes three I'm going to hurt whoever delivers my next meal, storm out of here, and get some answers.

The door opens and the woman who chewed out Archie is now all buttoned-up and tight-lipped. "We're going for a ride," she says, and I do not look at her as I pass.

The same black car that picked me up drives to Alexandria and parks outside a Popeye's Chicken off Duke Street.

"I need my gun," I say to the woman in the front seat, though I don't expect an answer. She swivels and hands me back my Glock. Guess it doesn't hurt to ask. The car leaves as soon as I climb out. I don't imagine I'll ever see the woman again.

A line of black clouds rolls in from the west, a chilly wind paving the way for it, so I pull up my jacket collar and enter the fast-food joint. Archie sits in a booth by himself, eating from a box of butterfly shrimp.

"I suspect he got 'em."

"Why?"

Archie wipes his fingers with a napkin, reaches down beside himself, pulls up a piece of paper encased in a plastic bag, and slides it across the booth to me. There are pictures of Archie himself from years back, and text detailing my relationship to him, from the time he was my fence up to when I disappeared with Risina to the Philippines.

"This was at the safe house in Memphis. When a couple of agents went in to look on Risina and your boy, and they was gone. Just this note, placed neatly on the middle of the bed."

"Sign of a struggle?"

Archie shakes his head.

"Anything out of place?"

He shakes his head again.

Before I ask another question, he interrupts. "He knew where the safe house was, he left that paper on me, we gotta assume he got 'em. How he did it? It's beyond me. But we'd've heard if she got away, right?"

"She was gonna run."

"What'choo mean run?"

"We said good-bye. That day."

"Well," Archie says. "There's no run in this game. You know that." He leans over and puts his finger on the photo of himself. "And I'm in it now, too, you see? 'Cause if recent events are any indication, Castillo's coming for my head next. That's why I brought you here, why we're eating at Popeye's in the middle of broad daylight. Why I'm eating some shrimps. I'm not gonna hide, Columbus. Not my style. He wants to come at me, well, that's what you want, too, right? Let's get the two birds lined up and lift a big stone."

"Castillo's left a bloody mess at every crime scene, but Risina and Pooley are snatched away with no sign of a struggle?"

"That's right."

"So he wants to use them in a bargain."

"I don't know about that."

I lean back. "Don't tell me to get in a mindset where they're already gone, or I swear to god, Archie, I'll come across this booth and knock your teeth out."

Archie smiles. "There he is."

Archie and I hole up at the Dupont Circle Hotel in D.C., registered under Archibald Grant. If Castillo wants to find us, we're going to make it easy. I try to picture Risina and Pooley in his possession, scared, chained, but my mind turns away from the image, a defense mechanism. As soon as the picture starts to form, a cloud of black ink overpowers it, like a squid scurrying away from a diver.

Archie emerges from the bathroom, looking younger than I last saw him, reverse-aging. The grief of his sister's death weighed him down, but now he is reborn.

"They been working you?" I ask.

"Like a dog. I have a half-dozen guns in my pool, and after these guys—what'd you call 'em?"

"Dark men."

"After the dark men saw the value of what you do, they just kept coming back to me. Third-party shit. They don't get they hands dirty, you know, they pay on time, and if one of my boys gets in a spot, that spot's removed. Know what I'm saying? Like it was never there. Whooosh." He slaps his hands together like one is a rocket blasting off from the other.

"Well, you look good," I say and I mean it.

"I wish to hell I could say the same for you, Columbus. You always had a way about you that I dug. Still do. But your step is a little slower."

"Thanks."

"I'm just saying."

"I just gave you a goddamn compliment."

"I know it. And I said thank you."

"No, you didn't. You lit right into me."

"Well, I apologize for that, then." He cracks a couple of beers from the minibar, hands one to me. I'm spread out across the sofa, so he spins the desk chair around to face me, puts his feet up on the small glass coffee table. "I got a feeling, Columbus. I got a feeling they's okay. I don't say that when I don't mean it. If he was gonna kill 'em, well, then, I think we'd've found 'em in the safe room with the paper like he'd done the others."

"That's what I said. And it's what scares me. He has something planned."

"That may be. We wait and see."

I look down at my hand and the beer bottle is empty. "I don't like playing defense, Archie. It's not my game."

"Your game is killing a man. It don't matter which side of the court you're on. You're gonna get another opportunity, Columbus. I promise you that. And when you do, you do your job."

He's right, but I can't help but feel like I've blown that chance, that Castillo had me on my heels before I set my feet. Of course, he also had the opportunity to put me down, and here I am.

Archie scans my face like a sculptor looking over a block of marble. "Why'd you do it?" he asks.

"Do what?"

"Take a shine to that lady? Bring a kid into the world?"

"We're gonna go there?"

"Oh, we're there, Columbus. We been there since you run off with her. You knew this day was coming. I *know* you didn't think you could outrun it. So why, then?"

"Why'd you let your sister take contracts?"

"So's I could keep an eye on her. But she was already in it, Columbus. And you saw what happened to her. You was there, man. So when I heard you'd run off with a woman, I thought, *not him. Not Columbus. He's too smart for that. He mustn't care for this lady a whit.*

"Then I heard she's *pregnant*. What? I said, *no, no, no. Not my man. Not him. No way.* And here you are. Goddamn. You more heartless than any of these other guns."

"You got an incredible bedside manner, Archie. You should've been a doctor."

"And you don't like to look at the truth."

"What d'you want me to say?"

"I want you to tell me why," he roars, the most emotion I've ever seen from him. "Why the fuck would you disrespect the job this way?"

I just stare at him, my face hot. "It's not about respecting the job or disrespecting the job. I met Risina and I didn't have a choice. She was in my life from that moment on. Pooley happened and I'm glad for it."

"Arrogance."

"You're a lot of fun."

"It's goddamn arrogance. And when they die, or if they're already dead, you're not going to feel sorrow. Only shame and disgust. I know. I know."

"You wanna yell at someone, Archie. Go yell at the mirror!"

He stands, and right then the phone rings. We look at each other like kids caught smoking behind the house, and then I hurry over to pick up the receiver.

"You know who I am?" asks Castillo.

"Yes."

"You want 'em back?"

"Yes."

"I bet you do."

I wait for more.

"You got people tracing this phone?"

"Just you and me," I answer.

"That's not true," he says. "It's never been just you and me."

"You wanna philosophize, take it to a bunch of assholes who'll listen. I don't give a fuck what's inside your head. I want the woman and the boy back, so tell me what I gotta do to get 'em."

He chuckles and it sounds like ice tumbling in a glass. "You know Pepperell, Massachusetts. There's a bridge there, one of the old covered ones like in the headless horseman. You and your black friend come. I hear any helicopters, see any cars, you'll be reading another tale about headless people, this time in the newspaper. You approach from the east. I'll come from the west. Don't fuck with me, Columbus. I want you buried. I don't care about anyone else. You for them, easy as that. Your friend can take them home."

"I watch them drive off, then we see?"

"Yes, yes. I don't care."

"When?"

"Tomorrow at midnight. I'll cut off their heads if you're one minute late," and the line goes dead.

D.C. to Pepperell, Massachusetts, is a seven-hour drive, so we set out before sunrise because I'm not going to risk any road obstructions delaying our arrival. Somewhere outside of New York, Archie asks if I know what I'm doing and I say yes. He asks why in the name of God Castillo picked a covered bridge in the middle of nowhere Massachusetts and I have an answer. It's simple, really. Pepperell is five minutes from the Waxham Juvenile Detention Facility where I spent five years of my life, from thirteen to eighteen, after my foster brother and I were convicted of killing our foster mother. His name was Pooley, too, and I loved him.

The covered bridge at Pepperell is the last landmark you pass from the outside world before you go into that hellhole and the first thing you see when you leave. For that reason, the bridge holds legendary status at Waxham.

You going to cross that bridge next week, ain't ya, Larry?

This boy been back and forth over that bridge three times already.

You ain't gonna see that bridge till you a man, son.

There is a story or two about boys who escaped Waxham and hid on top of the bridge as search dogs and police cruisers rolled underneath, but those might be apocryphal.

"He's showing me how well he knows me, how every detail of my life is his to exploit."

"Damn," says Archie. "So what's the plan?"

"I'm taking him at his word. I watch Risina and Pooley climb into this car with you, and he either hits me with a sniper bullet or he wants to fight at close range. I have a feeling it's the latter, because he's going out of his way to play a game. Popping me from afar doesn't fit. He'll want to have a conversation or try to set some combat rules and that'll be his mistake and I'll make him eat it. I'll agree to whatever he wants as long as my family is safe. As soon as they are, I'll kill him. If you're asking for a plan, that's my plan."

Traffic remains sparse and we arrive in Pepperell off Route 113 just after one. Eleven hours to kill. There's an old country store near the covered bridge with antiques and knickknacks and soaps and trinkets and we poke our heads in but Archie's about as comfortable there as a kid in a graveyard. I ask the clerk if he's seen a man with a funny accent and I imitate Castillo's voice but the woman behind the counter says *no, she'd've remembered that.*

The country store divides into a maze of rooms spilling with keepsakes and treasures, every surface covered with something to separate an old lady from her money. Archie tells me he's gonna go grab a smoke out at the car and I nod and drift. This must've been an old Victorian home at one point, someone grew up here, ate here, laughed here, cried here. It is a house with family secrets that now peddles junk. I fight an urge to grab a cigarette from Archie and burn it to the ground.

In the room next to mine, two men talk.

"If that were true, Father, we might as well throw in the towel."

"Now, now, don't talk that way, Sidney. I won't have it."

My heart beats faster. I know that voice.

"They can tell us 'no' this time and they can tell us 'no' the next time, but I'll outlast their 'no's, I can promise you that. Every time I turn around, they'll see my face, a smile on it, my hat in my hands, and I won't grovel or get angry."

I angle for the opening where the two rooms join so I can see the faces of the men in conversation.

"You'll wear them down with your smile?"

"That's it. That's it exactly. Because to the politicians, Waxham is just a dark name on the budget report, a necessary evil to be avoided. But I put a face on the place."

The two men are seated at a small glass table with white wire chairs, sipping coffee out of paper cups. They both have white hair.

One is dressed in denim jeans, a long-sleeve brown shirt, boots. The other is in the black suit and white clerical collar of a Catholic priest. His name is Father Steve. And though he has a few more wrinkles, his face looks the same as it did when I was a resident of Waxham. There might have been a warden, but Father Steve runs the place and though time there is hard, he was always firm and fair. He helped me get my first job after my release, packing beer trucks for his brother. As though he has an eye in the back of his head, he turns and looks at me, and for some reason I don't duck away or divert my eyes.

He nods at me, starts to look away, then perhaps recognition flickers in his eyes. I nod back, then head outside.

Archie waits by the car. I snatch the cigarette out of his hand and take a drag.

"Let's check out this fucking bridge," I say.

He looks at me sideways, then follows me up the road.

Dolce is a wood-fired Italian grill on Main Street in Pepperell. It promises authentic Italian cuisine and I do not argue with them as I order a steak sub. Archie seems annoyed with all of this—the white-bread town, the lack of strategy, the chicken panini in front of him. He pulls off the bread and picks at the meat.

The clock ticks.

Are they close to us right now? Miles away? A few hundred feet from this spot?

More likely Castillo is holding them in the back of a rental truck, on the move, so no one can hear them scream.

"Come on," I say to Archie. "Let's drive."

Maybe I'll get lucky and spot them before Castillo puts his plan in motion.

We arrive at the designated spot on the east end of the bridge, fifteen minutes before midnight. The sky is streaked with clouds so the moon peeks out only fleetingly, like a child in a window spying on the street.

We leave the car's headlights on, pointed across the bridge, but the darkness overwhelms the light, so it can only penetrate the bridge's mouth before it surrenders in defeat.

Archie props one foot inside the car while the other locates the pavement. His eyes work the darkness for any sign of danger.

I step a few paces toward the covered bridge and wait outside the opening, struggling to see anything beyond the opening at the other end. There are no lights other than our headbeams, no sound beyond our own breathing. The river itself seems to be holding its breath.

I thought about driving straight over the bridge with my lights out to erupt out the opening on the other side, ready to open fire on any movement or anything that looks remotely like Castillo, but I can't risk it, can't risk that he would just immediately pop my wife and child before I got to him. He isn't afraid to kill women and children. He's proved that.

I had all day to think about it and this is the only percentage play. I have to take the cards I've been dealt and stay in the game long enough to flip the table.

My eyes adjust to the night and some of the shapes inside the covered bridge ease into focus: the crossbeams in the ceiling, a bucket with a wooden handle on a pedestrian walking surface to the right of the road.

Fifteen minutes passes. Twenty.

A red light glows behind me. Archie with another cigarette.

Twenty-five minutes. Thirty.

"We got played," Archie says, the first words either of us have spoken since we got here. He takes another drag, his face a question mark, waiting for me to fold. I search the other side of the bridge for any interruption to the darkness but there's nothing. I don't understand. There's no game in this. There's—

Light blasts from the other side of the bridge, a couple of floodlights that wipe out the darkness, burning hot streaks into our retinas. It's blinding, the same effect as spraying dark paint over security cameras. The same effect I used in Paris with my camera bulb. Did he read about that one too?

My irises are so open from adjusting to the darkness that the strength of the lights is an assault, and my head starts to throb. The floodlights immediately shut off again, moments later. Pop, pop.

A figure stands at the far end of the tunnel dressed in black, walking toward me. My eyes are fried. I only see a blur, outlined in an orange, ghostly glow. My Glock is in my hand, automatic, like scratching an itch. The orange glow surrounding the blob turns blue, then red, then rises like a specter above the figure before fading. My eyes fight to adjust and my head throbs like thunder and the figure keeps coming, two hundred yards away, and now I can make out a second figure behind the first, not moving, a much larger shape, lower to the ground, like a man sitting on a sofa.

Still my eyes fight for the light as my brain tries to unscramble the input, put it into context, but the wires are crossed. The shape in front is on the bridge now, under the covered ceiling, but its arms make jerky movements, out of sync with its steady pace, a puppet with tangled strings. The second shape still hasn't moved but now my ears pick out a hum, a steady sound, an engine on idle. The sound locks my brain in, like discovering the keyword of a secret code, and the blurs become whole. A motorcycle. A man straddling it just outside the western entrance, sitting idle, helmet on.

Risina is the one walking toward me, persistent but irregular, like she's walking through snow, the footsteps unsure and tentative. Her chin is down and her hair covers her face like a curtain, her eyes cast down to concentrate on her footsteps. More disturbing are her arms, which spider toward her back at right angles, one above her head, one at her waist, a figure-8 of limbs.

"Columbus!" Archie bellows behind me, but I run to Risina as fast as my legs will carry me, inside the mouth of the covered bridge, my footfalls making tympanic echoes as I run and she walks and why isn't she running too and what are her arms doing and I'll kill this son-of-a-bitch, kill him and torture him and make him pay and still she turtles toward me, one foot locked and holding position until the next lifts, but I double her speed, triple it, and my gun hand is up and pointed over her shoulder at Castillo in the motorcycle helmet just watching us the way a scientist studies rats in a maze.

I'm about to fire a shot past Risina when she looks up for the first time and I see her mouth is gagged with a bandana in the colors of an American flag. Her eyes look horrified, traumatized as they find my face and it's as though, in that moment, she holds hope and defeat in equal measure.

Three more steps and I'm to her and she collapses forward and there is so much blood, my hands bathe in it. There's a knife stuck in her back, a serrated hunter's blade, the kind used to skin felled animals, deer, antelope, elk, before the hunter drags its carcass back to camp. A blood-soaked piece of paper is attached to it, another page from my file, another red stain of my history attached to a human being in an inhuman manner.

I ignore the paper and I think I'm screaming at Castillo on his motorcycle, my words punctuated with spit and hatred, echoing off the walls of the covered bridge, and the whole time I lay Risina on her side so as not to aggravate the knife's trauma and there is no sign of my son Pooley but I work the bit out of Risina's mouth and she says *it's not him, it's not him, it's not him* over and over.

Archie arrives beside us. I didn't hear him coming because my world is just Risina and pain and he's saying *oh man, oh man,* but I can't hear him.

"It's not him," Risina says again, losing steam, like a computer powering down.

"Go get him," Archie says, and my eyes narrow and my anger overwhelms me and I run, no, race at Castillo, smug on his bike, watching stoically. Fifty yards away, forty, closing, and my finger is on the trigger and it's not right, *it's not him,* she said, nothing is right, he's just sitting there, the motorcycle, a dirt bike is *putt, putt, putting,* not revving, no variation, and the only movement from Castillo is minimal. The shoulders flex up and down and I want to shoot from here, just fire a bullet through the helmet, but it's not right, it's not him.

I burst out of the western end of the Pepperell covered bridge and the moon has split open the clouds and the darkness is lifted and in those last few feet I see the rider's hands are tied to the handlebars with duct tape and his shoulders rock up and down, his attempts to loosen his wrists, and there's a muffled *mmmmmmm* sound behind the blacked-out visor of the helmet.

I rip it away, nearly snapping the motorcyclist's neck, and Father Steve's eyes stare back at me. His mouth is gagged with another bandana, this one a Spanish flag, and he's terrified and confused and he'll never have answers. He's just another poor player from my past who was discovered, exploited, and discarded by an assassin who is more concerned with possessing me than finishing me off.

"He, he, he, he, he told me he has a rifle and if I moved the bike, he would, he would . . ." but I stop paying attention because my senses are heightened now, and the forest and hill and covered bridge rack into frenzied focus so I can see individual branches, tree trunks, and nests of leaves. And then movement, high and to my right, a glint of moonlight off green-tinted binoculars and I know it's him, watching, enjoying.

"Get her to a hospital!" I scream over my shoulder at Archie, and he scoops up Risina like a groom carrying his bride across the threshold.

"I got her, go, go, go!" he yells back at the top of his lungs, the covered bridge his megaphone, and while he scampers back toward our car, I pull a knife from my ankle strap, slit off the duct tape in two quick swipes, and then knock Father Steve off the dirt bike. I don't have a chance to look at the instruments or take in the make and model of this bike, I just throttle it, spin in a 180 of disturbed dirt and leaves, and the tires find purchase and I shoot up the road at the hill like a bullet out of a rifle.

Castillo breaks from his surveillance post and sprints over a hill and I gun the bike toward him. I'm no expert rider and I'm reluctant to storm the bike into dark, unfamiliar woods at night, but if I have to, I will.

I don't have to.

As I break the horizon and crest the next hill, a dark SUV fires up and jolts forward. I crack my wrist, stomp through the gears, and chase forward. The wind cuts my eyes and bites my cheeks or maybe that's my hatred, made manifest.

The SUV slides into a ninety-degree angle and I do the same, a good two hundred yards behind. I nearly lay the bike on its side through the turn, aggressive for this road, and pop back up.

A monstrosity looms to my left and I realize it's the Waxham Juvenile Correctional Facility, built into the side of the hill, separated from the road I'm on by barbed wire and a mile-long clearing. Somewhere inside are boys awake after lights out, listening to this racket and wondering what the hell is happening out there, dreaming of life after eighteen.

My engine screams and I gain on the SUV, which plows ahead, black and faceless. It takes a sharp turn away from Waxham, away from the lights of my headbeam, so when I hit the same turn, I judge it on timing and feel. For a precarious second, I think the bike is going to lie all the way down and slide right out from under me, or take me with it in a tangle of leaves and limbs, but the tires hold and I'm upright again, but the brake lights ahead are gone. Just woods and shadows, and, as if in conspiracy with Castillo, the moon hides too.

This is country darkness. City dwellers don't understand country darkness. It's a black hole, sucking the light of my single headlight, rendered useless beyond a few feet.

I slow the bike as my head swivels from one side of the road to the other, and now I come upon an old-fashioned travel circle, the kind that splits off into four directions, north, south, east, and west.

I choose the second turn, south, for no reason other than instinct.

As with most of my choices since I read the name Castillo on the top of the page, my instincts are wrong.

CHAPTER

10

DO YOU WANT ME TO TELL YOU SHE LIVED?

Is that what you want to believe?

That when I gave up hope of finding the SUV, of catching Castillo, I turned around, discovered the hospital where Archie took Risina, burst through the emergency room doors, flagged down a nurse, and screamed "young woman, stabbed in the back!"

And she yelled "Room 23!"

And I sprinted down the corridor while orderlies and nurses in blue scrubs spun out of my way.

And when I got to the operating room, a smiling surgeon told me "she pulled through and is doing fine."

And I said "when can I see her?"

And he said "now."

And I rushed into her room and she was tired but awake and alert, on a recovery bed, and I poured her some water and put it to her lips and smothered her forehead with kisses and whispered "I'm so sorry, I'm so sorry."

Is that what you want to hear?

Will that make this easier for you?

Do you prefer the lie?

It's okay. Most people do.

So many shut their eyes and turn off the news and click off the page with the headlines about tragedy and death.

They want to believe in the sunsets and the goodness of humanity and the stories that progress to just endings.

Lies are popular and truth is the uninvited guest who spoils the party.

And what do you imagine that conversation sounded like in the recovery room?

"I'm so sorry. I'm so sorry."

"Pooley—"

"I don't—"

"My God . . ."

"I love you. I love you, Risina, and I will get him back. Look at me. I promise you. I will get him back."

And she sees it in my eyes and nods.

"And after this one, when Castillo is in the ground, when I've buried a bullet in his brain, after this one, we're going to run and we're not going to look back. We've done it once and we can do it again, dark men be damned, damn every last one of them, because we were egotistical to think we could do this and outrun the consequences. We were contemptuous of fate, of God, of nature, of the job, this life, and we have a chance to correct it, step off this bloody road, swim out of the undertow, and we can do it, we can really do it, Risina, this time we can do it."

And she looks at me, eyes brimming with love, and she puts a hand on my cheek and says *it's okay*. And she says my real name and *it's okay* again, and *shhhhhhhh*.

And then I pat her hand and say "Risina, I love you more than life itself. I loved you the moment I walked into that bookstore in Rome. I love you now and forever. And I'm going to hold you again, I'm going to be by your side forever. But first I have to go get our boy."

And she answers "Yes. Bring my son back to me."

Is that how you think it should go?

The version where the miracle doctors perform the miracle surgery and the serrated knife doesn't do any damage and the assassin's wife lives?

These lies are beautiful but illusory, fresh flowers placed on a grave.

CHAPTER

11

ARCHIE AND I STAND IN A BREAK ROOM OF A GOVERNMENT building in Boston. The room consists of a refrigerator, a commercial coffee maker, the kind with two pots, brown handle for regular, orange for decaf, and a small circular table with four chairs pushed up underneath it. The far wall is all glass, a window that faces the harbor.

I lean against its smooth surface, in a fog. The only thing keeping me upright is the thought of Pooley in Castillo's possession.

Archie is haggard, gray. The bounce in his step is gone. His smile, all those teeth, gone. He rubs his thumb over the back of his hand subconsciously. We haven't said two sentences to each other since the hospital.

He looks up, as though a puzzle piece just fell into place. "You told me once what Vespucci taught you. Said that to do this job, you have to make the connection so you can sever the connection. You remember telling me that?"

"I do."

"Well, I been thinking about that a lot since Ruby. You make the connection with your mark, right? You get inside his head, you feel his evil, you do the deed, you kill him, and then it's like you killed the bad part of yourself. That way, you can walk away free, shut of it, right? You cut out the cancer, and you get to walk away healthy. That it?"

"Yeah, that's it."

"Well, it's bullshit. Complete bullshit, Columbus. We don't get to walk away from what we do. There are ramifications, sacrifice, bloodshed—to us and everyone around us. There's a physical price, not just a mental one, a physical price. And here's the thing . . ." His lower lip sticks out, defiant. "Here's the thing. It's fair. It's the fair price for what we do."

I am in the fog and his words are just words because I cannot feel them right now.

"Awww, forget it. You don't need to hear this shit from me. I'm gonna go get some smokes."

He takes a step toward the door when a thirty-year-old white kid pokes his head in the room. "Uh, guys, we have something."

We follow him down a corridor. He has a woodwind voice, the affected nerd cadence from too many years in college labs. "So the blood thoroughly soaked the page to the point of unreadable, as you both know, and the problem is the page itself contained three different ink sources, or I shouldn't qualify them as ink since one of the sources is actually a lead pencil but you get the idea. Anyway . . . we scrubbed the blood using chemicals to reduce the organic content but our fear was it would also destroy some of the ink content and then we'd be guessing . . ." his words keep coming as we walk down what might be the longest hallway I've ever traversed. I think he's telling me they cleared Risina's blood off the paper that was attached to her back by the knife and were able to recover the data underneath. I think, but I'm not sure. I just nod and keep walking and wait for this prick to shut up.

We reach a dark room with a couple of other analyst-types inside and there are hi-resolution monitors and the page itself on a light board. The blood is faded so the page looks as though it were smeared with rust. The ink and pencil underneath are darkened and enhanced so each letter looks like it is made of toothpicks.

It's a page about the Columbus Textile Company warehouse, site of my first kill, my foster father, a man named Mr. Cox. The tale told on this page is that Vespucci—my first fence and the probable source for most of Aiza's file—Vespucci hid a gun and bullets inside the warehouse, brought my abuser and me to the location, told us only one of us would walk out of the building the next morning, and shut the door. It said I found the bullets and shot Mr. Cox and then joined Vespucci's roster as a contract killer.

But the paper is inaccurate. I never found the bullets. The fight only lasted a few minutes. I wrestled Mr. Cox for the gun, pistol-whipped him, then picked up an old sewing machine and dropped it on his head. There was no long struggle, no problem to solve. To this day, I don't know where Vespucci hid those bullets. I killed Cox in the first two minutes and then spent the night with the body until they opened the doors.

"What's this mean?" asks the kid.

The Columbus Textile Company warehouse is exactly how I left it, minus the dead body of Mr. Cox. Whoever owns the property has done nothing to sell it or improve it, and I wonder if the deed for the place is lost and forgotten. The dark men back at the office wanted to talk strategy and tactics, wanted to draw up a plan and send in men in ghillie suits in case Castillo is here, but I told them no, I would come here alone and no one there wanted to contradict me. I assume it was something in my eyes.

I take a couple of steps inside the door and even though I only spent one night in this place, it's as familiar to me as my face in a mirror. I've thought about this place a million times. It is in my name. The life chose me here. The dust is thicker, the blood is gone, but the old heavy sewing machines remain on tables and I can feel the weight of them in my hands.

I have my pistol out but he's not going to sucker-punch me. He wants a fight.

A phone rings to break the silence. It vibrates on a table next to the sewing machines, sending up flurries of dust motes, then rings again, obstreperous, demanding. I cross to it, eyes jumping. I know I'm being watched. Again.

I hesitate before picking up the phone, worried it will stop ringing, a small part of me hoping it does. I push that thought from my head, slide my finger across the face, and place it against my ear.

"Daddy?" and I'm on my knees without thinking like someone took a baseball bat to the back of my legs. In that moment, I know why all religions put you on your knees to pray, to lower your head, to ask for mercy and forgiveness.

I fight to keep my voice steady, positive. "Hi, baby. Hi, Pooley. Hi, son. How are you?"

"Where are you, Daddy?"

"I'm here, baby. I'm right here."

"Where's Mommy?" and I have to lower the phone because my chest heaves, wracked with silent sobs, a scream contained, my insides destroyed. I'm going to kill this man. Before I die, I will kill Castillo and I will need no connection to live peacefully with it.

I put the phone back to my ear and concentrate on keeping despair out of my voice. "Mommy's resting, baby."

"Okay. You come home?"

"Yes, baby, I'm coming home."

"Okay, bye," he says in the way kids do on the phone. When they're done, it's over, bye.

Castillo's voice replaces Pooley's. "Cute boy. Smart."

I don't answer.

"I like the way you answered him. Mommy's resting. That was a good one."

Nothing from me.

"You want to see him, Columbus?"

"Yes."

"Alive or dead?"

"Alive."

"Then why oh why'd you come after me? What did you think would happen?"

"I'm going to kill you."

He clucks his tongue. "Ahhhh. Okay. I see. I might have been forgiving. I had heard the name Columbus for a long time. The great Columbus. He's a Silver Bear, they'd say. He's the best in the world. Politicians? The one in California? That was Columbus. The crime boss in Paris? Columbus. Everywhere I went, Columbus. And it was so perfect. So perfectly American. Columbus, killer of men and women. No mark too protected, too secure. Once a name is at the top of a contract . . . *pssst, pssst* . . . that name is scratched out."

My face is hot as a griddle. I let him keep talking.

"So I said to Aiza. I said, 'Find out everything you can about Columbus?' 'Why, Castillo. It will only cause trouble for me, for you.'" He imitates Aiza like he's a high-pitched old fool. "I said to that fat fuck, do it. I want to know everything about him. I want to study him. I want to understand him. I want to know all of his secrets. And I learned so much. I changed the way I completed a contract to be more like Columbus. I changed my haircut, the clothes I wore, the way I lived. I didn't need the surplus. I didn't need friends, people in my life, nice clothes, fancy cars. The money wasn't important. You taught me that. It was the job. Only the job."

Above me, condensation on an old HVAC pipe pearls and falls, over and over, *drop, drop, drop.*

"And then what does Aiza uncover for me? Columbus, the perfect Columbus, the Silver Bear Columbus, has a wife and child. *No,* I thought. *This cannot be. Not this man. Not the man I changed my whole life to become.* Columbus is an ascetic. 'Are you sure,' I asked and I pored over the report again and again. Maybe this was some kind of inventive angle, a new play Columbus made? No, no, the paperwork told me. He's just another man who disrespects the job."

The water on the pipe drops again. *Drop, drop.* It hits me on the back of the head.

"Abe Mann," I say.

"The congressman, yes," and I can hear the smile in his voice as he knows that I know.

"You set this up. From the beginning. You put your own name on the top of the page. You initiated the contract. Like him. Another event from my past. You wanted me to come after you."

"I first thought about reaching you through Archibald Grant," he says. "Aiza thought you still fulfilled contracts for him. But no, that wasn't true. These men you *are* working for, they were easy to manipulate. Lavender. Cargill. I worked hard to get my name on their lips. And the beauty . . . you would've understood this years ago when you were still vital . . . the beauty was they never knew they were being used. They thought it was their idea to put a hit on me."

"Mann wanted to die," I say.

"I just want to own you and destroy you," Castillo answers.

"Okay, Angelo, let's finish this rather than cluck on a phone like a couple of assholes."

"Ahhh, you know my real name."

"Your mother told me."

"What's yours?"

"My real name is go fuck yourself."

"I'm going to get you to say it."

"Are you?"

"You'll tell me. When the time comes, you'll tell me."

"Where do you want to meet?"

"The answer is in that room. Keep this phone on. We'll speak soon."

He hangs up. My knees hurt but I'm too tired to stand. I look around, collect my thoughts, and center on the task at hand. I have to find the next page from my file.

I didn't move too far the first time I was inside this warehouse. I fought Pete Cox, I won, and I spent the rest of the night lying on my back, staring at the ceiling, waiting for the sun to come up. I climb to my feet and move to the spot where I killed him.

It doesn't take me long to find the paper.

Jake, Risina, Pooley. Waxham, the dark men, the Columbus Textile Company, Abe Mann. All of my history. He wants to own it for himself, to possess me. I've spent so many assignments making connections with my marks so I could sever the connection, and it hits me now, it's been right here all along, though I didn't see it.

He's making the connection with me.

The page lies on a table in the empty space a sewing machine once occupied, the sewing machine I picked up and dropped on Pete Cox's head.

He already knows my real name. He just wants me to say it so he can own it too.

<hr />

Archie asks if I have a plan. I have no plan.

Archie asks if I want some other guys. I don't want other guys.

Archie asks if I'm thinking clearly. I'm not thinking clearly.

Archie asks what he can do to help. He can do nothing to help.

I haven't had time to mourn. I focus on the task at hand.

It is the oldest human story. I must sacrifice myself so my son may live.

I give Archie the paper and he turns it over and over in his hand, corner to corner to corner to corner. "This was your mother?" he asks.

I nod.

The page contains an article about a black woman found dead behind a Sohio gas station, a knife in her ribs. Her name was LaWanda Dickerson. She had recently given birth to a boy and was forced to give that child to the State. The photo accompanying the article shows a mugshot of LaWanda Dickerson, my mother, with a caption that explains she was picked up more than once for prostitution. The paper also contains a drawing of the Sohio station's property, as though from an aerial view, with a red X showing where the body was found, in an alley, near a dumpster, close to a thick woods, away from the road.

"He's taking it all the way to my birth. To the place my mother died."

"You went after *his* mother. Or I should say you tried to get to him through his mother. Seems like he isn't taking kindly to that."

"No."

"Well, what you gonna do?"

"He told me to keep the phone on. I'm going to drive to the gas station where my mother was murdered and wait for him to call."

Archie throws up his blinker, takes the highway exit, and pilots us into a strip mall: a liquor store, dry cleaners, frozen yogurt, an electronics shop. He cuts the engine, looks me over.

"You got what you need?"

I nod.

"Guns?"

"I'm loaded."

"I'm gonna give you this car."

"What're you gonna do?"

"I'm gonna get me a froyo. Call Uber. Go check into a hotel and pay cash until either you dead or he is. Cat's killed everyone else you run with so I think I'll sit the rest of this nonsense out."

He dislodges the key and holds it up to me. We both sit inside the car, neither making a move to climb out.

"I'm sorry about your woman. I really am. I *do* know how it feels. And I want you to know I believe in you. And my door will always be open to you when this is finished. But part of me. Part of me, Columbus, hopes you never come through that door again. And I don't mean I hope you die by this punk's hand. I just mean I hope you get your boy back and you finish what you meant to years ago. You get out, away, gone." He stops, frustrated. "But . . . I look at you and I know that won't happen."

"Yeah? Is that what you see?"

"I see a killer," he says and opens the door, leaving the keys on the seat. I watch him through the windshield. He enters the frozen yogurt shop, grabs an empty cup, and heads over to the machines.

He doesn't look back at me.

Death is ugly.

Finding peace at the end is the biggest lie we tell ourselves.

I drive a two-lane highway toward the intersection where the Sohio station meets the Virginia woods. I have no file. I've never been to this spot. Beyond the crude drawing on the page left at the Columbus Textile Company, I'm blind, alone.

The sun drops like it is weighted down, stones in its pockets. The phone in my passenger seat remains mute. I am cold, hard, and unfeeling. If he's going to present me with a fresh horror, my dead son, I will be immune to it. I play it in my mind on a continuous loop so I will be numb. If part of his game is to shock me with Pooley's corpse, he will not gain the satisfaction.

The miles to this confrontation are new and the same.

I want to tell you the truth about what happens. All of it. Every detail.

I reach the parking lot of the Sohio station just after eleven at night. The place is dark, empty. The woods behind it are from a Grimm's faerie tale, foreboding, forbidden.

As soon as I kill my engine, the phone rings.

"Welcome," Castillo says. His voice sounds close. He could whisper and I'd hear it.

"Get on with it," I answer.

Up the road, headlights blink on and off. "You see me?"

"I see you."

"What do you feel right now? I want to know."

"Nothing."

"That's not true. You feel what I feel. Anticipation."

"I'm through talking."

"Your mother was murdered here. Around behind the building, not far from where you sit now. She was a whore. You are the progeny of a whore. Her blood spilled while you were still in diapers, already someone else's problem, yes? And you don't have to tell me how that makes you feel because I know. Killing is your birthright. You were born into blood. And I know your secret, Columbus. I know your secret because I am you and you are me.

"You *like* it. You've always liked it. Before you claimed your right to kill, you were nothing. Killing gave you your life. It gave you your nature. And you tell yourself it's a business, and you tell yourself you do it because you're the best at it, but that's the lie. You would do it anyway. You do it because you enjoy it. You are the antagonist in your own life story. You, a hero? That's the lie."

I don't respond. I'm not sure the phone is in my hand or Castillo's voice is in my head. He talks, but I hear my own voice coming back to me.

"I am you," he repeats, meting out the syllables like they're a punishment. "And you are me."

"Get on with it!" I rage. "Get the fuck on with it!" The sound is a tidal wave and I wonder if Castillo can hear it up the road without the phone.

His voice remains calm. "The test Vespucci designed for you, the test that made you finally claim your birthright, it was a flawed design, wouldn't you say? I mean he puts you in a warehouse, he provides you with an enemy you despise, and he did something very unique. I was thrilled to read about it. He hid the bullets. In his mind, you would have to scrape over the gun and then search for the bullets and then wrestle for the weapon. A death match. A true death match.

"But you gamed the system. You didn't care about guns or bullets, you just cared about killing. The contest was over before it began. Have you wondered what would have happened if you'd played it out? I have."

"I haven't wondered. I would've killed Cox no matter the rules Vespucci laid out. I'm a killer. He was a coward. Simple as that. It would have shaken out the same."

"And what am I? Killer or coward?"

"It won't matter soon."

"Tell me your name."

"Columbus. No other name matters."

He sits for a long moment, chewing on that. "Are you ready?"

"I'm ready."

"Why haven't you made a move to come after my car here? You know where I am." He flashes his lights on and off again to emphasize the point.

"Because I don't know where my son is."

"And here is the surprise. I don't either."

The hair on the back of my neck stands at attention as gooseflesh sprouts on my arms. "What?"

"I was intrigued by your test. Vespucci's death match at the Columbus Textile Company warehouse. I've never been challenged like that, not against a professional such as yourself. When I read about it, I imagined the two of us in that warehouse, the gun between us, the bullets hidden. Do you know I found them? The bullets were still there, tucked inside a light fixture on the second-floor catwalk, preserved in time as though they'd been installed behind museum glass. In fact, they're loaded in my gun now.

"So here is the death match. Castillo versus Columbus. The young up-and-comer against the old man who thought he could have a wife and kid and there would be no repercussions."

Get on with it, get on with it, get on with it, I chant in my head like a soldier waiting for his troop transport to hit the beach and drop the gate.

"I asked your son, Pooley, if he knew how to play hide-and-seek. I told him an hour ago to get out of the car, run into the woods and hide. I told him not to make a sound, not even if his daddy called out to him. I told him there would be a big prize at the end of it.

"So, Columbus, my question is . . . can you get to him before me?"

———

I hear his car door slam right after mine and with no sound to interfere, his footsteps clop across the pavement as loud as jackhammers but I don't notice. We're two hundred yards apart, running parallel, toward the woods behind the gas station. I cross the spot where my mother's body was disposed of all those years ago, and dash across fifty yards of unexposed grass between the gas station and the tree line.

Shots ring out to my left and a pair of bullets chew into the ground, one plugs into the earth no more than a foot from me, and the other sails high, striking a tree trunk before sending splinters of shrapnel, and I run with my hands up in some kind of useless primal reaction to protect my face, and then I am in the no-man's-land of the woods. I did not blindly return fire because I have only thirty-six bullets and for once I have no idea how many I will need.

My paternal urge is to call out to my son. "Pooley! It's Daddy! Come to my voice!" but I bite those thoughts down because finding the prize is far less important than finding my enemy first. I don't know if he has night-vision goggles like he had at the Pepperell covered bridge or an arsenal of weapons but I doubt it. I think he wants to beat me on the battlefield, one on one, no advantages. It's an old tradition picked up from the animal kingdom, the two dominant males rip and tear and claw at each other until one is dead and the other returns to its clan, the undisputed leader.

I find a thick trunk and put my back to it to catch my breath after that sprint across the open field. I only have one pistol out in my right hand; I need the other as a kind of scout. If I'm going to pick my way through this thicket at night, I need it out in front of me to warn me of any low-hanging branches.

I don't know what Pooley is wearing, which clothes this bastard dressed him in, and the half-second it might take me to decide if the fabric I see belongs to Castillo or Pooley might cost me my life.

The woods hum, leaves rustle, the wind whistles, and nocturnal predators enjoy the hunt. I have to move as soon as my heartbeat normalizes, my breath regulates, and I can begin the dual challenge: search and evade. I listen, listen, listen for any anomalies in the natural hum, take one big breath and push out from the tree trunk.

Where might Pooley hide? I don't think he would walk deep into the woods. He's still a toddler and his hiding places are puerile, unimaginative. Maybe he found a spot behind a trunk somewhere and fell asleep or will soon give up and call for help.

It's warm enough to shed my shirt. My dark skin will be less reflective than the threads of my gray sweatshirt. If I get some scrapes and bruises, so be it.

I angle to my left, where Castillo's car is parked, where the shots came from, where he most likely entered the woods. I stay in the thicket, two hundred feet from the road, deep enough so if any cars pass or headbeams sweep my way, I won't be illuminated. I can't imagine Pooley entered much farther but I don't know exactly what Castillo told him, how much he scared him, or how much he even understood. We'd play hide-and-seek at the apartment and he would hide in a corner in plain sight for Chris'sakes. *Where's Pooley? Have you seen Pooley?* And he'd giggle like he was fucking David Copperfield.

Once, he hid in the bathtub after covering himself with pillows, like pillows in the bathtub wouldn't be a tipoff, but that's not how his mind works. If they can't see me, I must be gone.

I hear a branch snap somewhere in the darkness to my left but farther into the woods, and maybe I miscalculated, maybe Pooley did try to press farther into the trees. I told him once to run to his room and get on his PJs and when I went upstairs twenty minutes later, he was on the floor, naked, playing with stuffed animals. "I forgot," he told me by way of explanation, so maybe Pooley went to hide and forgot what he was playing and is tossing sticks around.

I move trunk to trunk to trunk, trying to keep my body small, tucking it up against each swath of bark as I pass.

I see him.

A shape to my left, ducking underneath branches, using the same technique as I am, propelling forward from trunk to trunk like a bee touching flowers. He doesn't spot me. It's full dark and he's wearing black clothes and I position myself for a clear shot. I aim for his head, pressure the trigger, but Pooley pops out from a flat spot on the ground, branches and leaves flying, pillows in a bathtub, and yells with delight, "Pop! Pop!"

Castillo jerks his head at the sound and sees me, sees both of us. We form a triangle, Castillo, Pooley, and me. I fire and he fires, guns cracking, legs churning, dirt flying, closing, closing, closing, and Pooley spills backward as Castillo and I crash into each other nearly on top of him.

Teeth and blood and elbows and pain.

"Run, Pooley, run!" I scream and as confused as he is, he hears his father's voice, turns, and scampers away, shrieking at a pitch only a child can make. I focus on Castillo, I can see his eyes bulge, but I hear a *splash*, and both of us look over as my son disappears fully clothed into a pond.

Castillo paws at my wrists, so I drive an elbow into his throat and crawl toward the water. I try to horse-kick him in the side of the head but I don't have time to see if the blow lands. I know kids can drown in less than a minute.

I make it to the bank of the pond, which is the size of a swimming pool and no Pooley, no thrashing at the surface, he's gone, somewhere underneath. I climb to my feet to dive into the pond, but at the same time Castillo roars and leaps for my back. We tangle, hit the dark water at the same time, and disappear underneath.

<hr />

I am the son of a whore and the mistake of a politician. I killed my first human being at the Columbus Textile Company warehouse when I was eighteen. I have killed many since. I murdered my dad with my bare hands. I am a contract killer. I am a bad man.

I am also a husband and I am a father.

And I am not going to die tonight.

Castillo's struggle is his mistake. A fisherman's son should know the way to pull a catch into the boat is to tire the fish out. Under the water, I relax while he flails, I make myself compact while he whips, I concentrate while he rages. And when I sense his strength weaken, when I feel he wants to try for the surface, I hold him. I can't see a thing in the green muck of this pond, but I hold him. He kicks and bends as he realizes what is happening, but I hold him. I hold him with every muscle in my body, and I will hold him either until he dies or I do.

From our mouths, two bubbles form and start upward. Above our heads, they merge and join together like twin cells bonding, and they stay that way until they break the surface. First one half gives way, then the other.

Pop, pop.

I crawl out of the pond like an evolutionary creature, a fish with legs, and hoist my filthy, grimy, bone-tired bag of bones on to the bank, sucking air in greedy gulps. I have to go back, have to hit the water again, have to find Pooley, but I can't until I refill my lungs. Just a few breaths, just enough to give me the strength to search. How long has it been since he splashed into the water? I have no idea.

Behind me, I hear a weak "Daddy?"

Pooley is there, shivering, his back to a tree trunk, his hands around his knees, the same position he takes in the bathtub. Water drips off of him and cascades to the earth.

I crawl to him and cradle his head in my hands and put my dirty lips to his forehead and I cry.

EPILOGUE

SHE CHANGED HER HAIR, DYED IT BLACK, CUT IT OFF SO it covers her ears, maybe a little longer in back.

She sits in a back booth, so I almost don't see her, and when Pooley and I approach, she doesn't stand. Pieces of a torn napkin are on the table.

Pooley has no problem sliding into the booth and scooting over near the wall. A waitress comes by, takes our coffee order, and hands a coloring book and a small pack of crayons to my son. "Ooooh," Pooley says and goes to work.

"Thanks for doing this," I offer, though I should have rehearsed something better.

"I'm not doing this for you. I'm doing it for him," Jake says.

"Where's AJ?"

"With my mother."

Pooley colors a leprechaun blue, his pot of gold red. I tousle his hair, touch his head so I will remember the feel of it on my skin.

"Are you sure about this?"

"What choice do I have?" she answers.

"You can say 'no.'"

"And leave him with you?"

"I can find someone else."

"No, I want him. I want to take him. To keep him safe. He deserves better than you."

"Jake—"

She levels her eyes at me. "What?" Sharp.

"No one will come for you again."

"You don't know that."

"I do."

"How?"

"Because I won't allow it."

"You can't know that. You've tried before."

"Sure I can."

She begins to argue further, but understanding hits. Her eyes soften.

I turn to Pooley, squeeze him into me. "Hey, buddy, hey. Look at me. Did you say hello to Jacqueline?"

"Hel-lo."

"She's gonna babysit you for a little bit."

"Where are you going, Daddy?"

"Not far, son."

"With Mommy?"

"Yes. With Mommy. But we'll be back soon, okay? Look at me. Yeah? You know what Daddy looks like?"

"Da-ad."

"That's right. Okay." My voice cracks but I don't try to mask it. "I'm gonna go now. You be good for Jacqueline. Okay. I'll see you again soon but you remember what Daddy looks like."

"Okay, Daddy."

"I love you." I choke on the word. "I love you."

"I love you, Daddy."

I rise from the booth on shaky legs. "Thank you," I mouth to Jake, but I can't look at her. I keep my eyes on the door.

"Copeland!" I hear her call out behind me, but I can't turn back now.